# The Fall of Jake Hennessey

P.J. MacLayne

# Acknowledgements

As always, thanks go to **K.M. Guth**, for her cover design and other graphic assistance. I never go wrong with giving her the freedom to let her creativity loose on my covers.

To Cornelia Amiri, for encouraging me to keep working on this story and share it with a wider audience.

And to Angela Pryce of Angela Pryce Editing, for her sharp eyes and gentle way of pointing out my errors.

*For my brothers and sisters, including my brothers and sisters-in-law, whose support comes in many forms.*

# Chapter 1

Caged in its gold setting, the deep-green emerald glowed in the dim light. Jake didn't stop to admire the ring before slipping it into the hidden pouch on his waistband. There'd be time for that before the new owners claimed the prize. It wasn't a stunning ring, but its ties to the French monarchy made it priceless to a collector.

First, he needed to cover his tracks. The Gordons, the occupants of the suite, shouldn't return from dinner for another half hour, but Jake wanted to be gone long before that. Sometimes getting out was harder than getting in.

He'd lifted a master keycard from a front desk agent and slipped a teenage boy five bucks to knock the security camera out of place. The security guard had been called to deal with an overflowing bathtub on the fifth floor, also courtesy of the master key.

The hotel had changed the default combination for the safe. Not a show-stopper, but Jake's goal had become more of a challenge and time-consuming. He'd had to unscrew the two fasteners from the front plate to reveal the locking mechanism. Next, using a hook pick and tension bar, he'd slipped the tumblers into the unlocked position and opened the safe's door to reveal the contents.

The cash was tempting and untraceable. Jake couldn't resist slipping one bill from the middle of the pack and tucking it into his pants pocket. However, his eyes had focused on the small, locked jewelry box.

Jake had feared he'd run into an electronic case, like those used to transport guns, but this container turned out to be old-fashioned and easy to open. Carved from dark brown wood and imbedded with ivory in a floral and vines pattern, the box was its own piece of art. Jake would leave it behind to make it less obvious anything was missing. He regretted having to abandon it. It might have earned him a hefty bonus.

With the ring tucked away, he reversed the order of his work: re-locked the jewelry box and returned it to the safe, closed the safe's door and made sure it locked, refastened the front plate, and shut the panel that covered the device.

All that remained was his escape. He opened the door a crack and pressed his ear to the opening. In this case, silence wasn't golden. He wished for a noisy group of travelers to come by, masking his exit. Better yet, the confusion caused by a blackout. Neither happened.

The deep voice of Roger Gordon flowed down the corridor. Jake was trapped with no way out. The suite had more hiding places than a standard room, but he wasn't a small man and wouldn't fit behind the sofa or in the closet. The ninth-floor room didn't have a balcony, and Jake hadn't brought a parachute.

There were other voices, ones he didn't recognize, but were relaxed and non-threatening. A door opened and closed, followed by silence. He had to risk it. He tucked the plastic gloves he wore into his jean's pocket and, as casually as if leaving his own room, he widened the crack with his shoulder and entered the hall, his phone in his hand. It was turned off, but the security cameras wouldn't catch that detail.

The cameras could track him throughout the hotel, so he did the obvious. He headed for the lobby, waved at the front desk clerk, and went outside, ostensibly for a cigarette. Jake didn't smoke, but the fresh air helped take the edge off his nerves. Plus, there were a couple of pretty ladies to flirt with and a trash can for his plastic gloves. Next stop would be the bar, a drink, and hopefully friendly company to distract him from the inevitable hangover left behind by the adrenalin rush he'd experienced. He wouldn't be in the clear until he checked out in the morning, but he congratulated himself on a successful mission. In a few days, the ring would reach its new owners and a fat bundle of cash would pad his slim savings.

His new venture was doomed before it even got off the ground. Jake pushed the binder of real estate flyers across the desk towards the agent and rubbed his chin. Was the stubble he cultured getting too long? In this game, appearances were half the battle. "Sorry, Sarah," he said, reading her name off the ID on her lapel. "But these are boring. Ranch-style houses all look the same to me. I'm plotting to tackle a project with personality."

If Sarah held out on him, he'd have to find another way to get to his goal. But he had time. He was lying low after the last theft and hadn't caught wind of anyone else interested in this target. "Boring" described the town of Oak Grove and everyone who lived in it. That included the petite, brown-haired lady sitting across from him, making her easy prey. He fluttered his eyes and leaned in. "Don't you have anything interesting listed? I swear I spotted a Victorian or two when I stopped to buy gas."

Until three days ago, Jake hadn't known a Victorian from a ranch from a hole in the ground. But he'd done his research and now could spout the basic lingo. It was all part of the game. He played to win.

His question got the hoped-for response. Sarah's eyes brightened, and she reached for a second binder. "I assumed you wanted quick flips, Mr. Hennessey. My apologies. If you are looking for a house with character, we have those, too. Of course, the nicest ones aren't for sale, but we have several older homes available." She flipped through the leaflets and stopped at one. "Is this more what you're looking for?"

Jake allowed his fingers to trail over hers as he reached for the book. A little flirting never hurt. She didn't pull away. A good sign, as was the slight blush that reddened her cheeks. He pretended to study the picture of the house she'd picked out, although it wasn't what he imagined. It sat squeezed between two other homes, and he valued his privacy. "Do you mind?" he asked, but didn't wait for her permission before turning the page.

Sarah didn't object. Good. That put him in control. Besides, he'd decided which house he wanted several days ago. It had looked empty, but he hadn't spotted a For Sale sign. Still, he'd picked this nondescript woman as his agent for a reason: her friendship with Harmony Duprie. Jake had spent a week stalking Duprie, determining her habits, and figuring out how to get close to her.

Rumor claimed that Duprie owned a rare 1777 edition of the English translation of The Three Musketeers. Another tidbit of gossip reported that a certain unscrupulous computer mogul on the west coast was in the market for the book. Jake normally worked in fine jewelry, but the challenge intrigued him.

Not to buy and sell the book or act as an agent between the two. He lived for the danger of a well-planned heist.

He flipped through several more pages. "Nothing's grabbing my attention." He closed the binder. "Maybe another time."

"We get new listings every week," Sarah said. "If you give me a contact number, I can alert you when something interesting hits the market."

Jake shook his head. "Nothing against you, Sarah, but my company enforces strict rules about handing out our numbers. Privacy concerns, you know. But if your agency has a website, I'll check it." He adjusted the sleeves of his tailored suit and flashed a practiced smile. "If you have a business card, I can reach out to you directly."

The excuse worked. It always did, especially with salespeople who saw it as a path to a big sale later. "Of course!" Sarah pulled a card from the holder on her desk and handed it to him. "My advice is to check every few days. Buyers from Pittsburgh and Cleveland are interested in our small town's lower real estate prices. The best deals get snapped up right away."

Jake took the card with his left hand and offered his right for a shake. When she shook it, he held hers for a second too long. The art of flirting had saved him a time or two.

He left the office more confident in his plan. A few adjustments and it would work. The book would be his for the taking. He grinned as he climbed into the rented car and headed south towards Pittsburgh. A room in a fleabag hotel waited for him there, under one of his alias names, but it was better than sleeping in a grocery store parking lot.

❋ ❋ ❋

Jake waited four days to return. He put his time in McKeesport to good use, making friends in run-down bars—easy enough to do with the money to buy drinks—and researching the job duties of a librarian. Despite her silly hairdo, instinct told him there was more to Duprie than the bun and thick glasses showed. How else would a small-town old maid have the resources to indulge in the expensive hobby of collecting rare old books?

The librarians at the Pittsburgh facility were more helpful than he expected. He spent one morning pretending to read business magazines to get a feel for the daily routine. The next day, he tracked one little old lady as she worked at the front desk and talked to the customers. He followed a pair of younger librarians to a nearby restaurant and listened to their gossip as they ate lunch. They discussed the latest popular TV show, but he also picked up a few choice pieces of their lingo. He'd remember to call the customers 'patrons' and the bookshelves 'stacks.'

The terminology would come into play later. But, he wasn't ready to woo the lady yet. A return trip to the real estate office topped his list

* * *

After the fourth house, Jake suspected Sarah's smile remained on her face out of habit, not happiness. "It would be better to tear down that last place and start over," he said.

"Sorry about that," Sarah said. "The listing is new, and I hadn't had the chance to see it yet. Thank you for catching me when the front step broke."

The almost-mishap had earned Jake bonus points for playing hero and given him a moment of enjoyment. When Sarah loosened up, her smile became less stiff and her eyes brighter. And it was never a bad thing to hold a lady in his arms. Jake's normal female companions were more interested in the booze or the buds he provided. Many of them spoke glowingly of his physical attributes, but he didn't trust their judgment.

He worked hard to stay in shape. Most people in the

business were slight in stature and able to worm their way through tight places. He had to make up for his size with his strength, dexterity, and magician-like sleight-of-hand skills. Also, his ability to read people's body language and use the knowledge to manipulate them. Some jobs, like this one, required all those techniques.

But his plans for the night were easy. He'd overheard Sarah discussing meeting up with her friends, including Duprie. He'd show his face, drink a beer, and then head back to the fleabag motel he'd found in McKeesport. It was a way to break the ice. No pressure.

※ ※ ※

The Pink Flamingo had an interesting decor for a small northern town. The faded plastic flamingo in the front window may have been pink at one time, but the sun had bleached it almost white. Once inside, Jake stood and studied the setup before proceeding past the dining area's pink booths and to the bar in the back. The feminine laughter coming from that direction assured him he'd found the right place. He took off his jacket and laid it on the stool beside him to deter any unwanted companions.

He wanted to be seen by one lady in particular. In the cloudy reflection of the mirror behind the bar, he had trouble determining which of two ladies in the group of four was Duprie, because they looked like sisters. But the brown hair worn in a bun was the giveaway. Once he identified her, he turned his focus to his beer and to the basketball game on the TV.

At least to outward appearances.

He was alert to her presence when the four women passed by on their way out. She seemed as willing to ignore him as he was to pretend that he didn't notice her. That situation would change when he was ready. It surprised him Sarah didn't stop and say hello, but perhaps she kept her work life separate from her night with her friends. Or, he flattered himself, she didn't want the competition for his affections. That worked well with his plan. The groundwork had been laid.

He used the drive back to McKeesport to look for flaws in the plan. The quiet ones were the ones to watch out for, and Duprie qualified. But until he got closer to her, he wouldn't know what surprises she held. He looked forward to finding out.

❋ ❋ ❋

Jake had figured out her schedule, so he didn't need to rush back to Oak Grove after he checked out of the motel. He'd found one for the same price that was cleaner and closer, off the interstate north of Pittsburgh. It would save him gas and time, and let him get more sleep. He intended to ignore Duprie for a day, but after taking a second shower in the bathroom with no roaches, he was bored. All the room's TV offered were soap operas or the news channels.

He planned to 'accidentally' bump into her on her way out of the library after work. But the hot showers, the fresh sheets and the droning of the news anchor lulled him into sleep.

He awoke with a jerk and a curse. The sun forcing its

beams through the thin curtains assured him he hadn't lost the entire day. He didn't have time for another shower, which he would have relished. It would take him several days to feel clean again.

The drive to Oak Grove restored his good humor. Driving always did. Sometimes, he considered becoming a truck driver, but that wouldn't supply the adrenalin rush of successfully pulling off a heist. And truck drivers were on the top of cops' suspect lists for crimes along major highways. Besides, he sought an opportunity to make this a two-for-one deal. There was talk about a jewelry exhibit at Fallingwater, a historical site north of Pittsburgh. There'd been no announcement about which collection would be displayed, but any of the Rockefeller groupings contained pieces worth his attention.

Her car didn't occupy its normal spot when he reached the library. It was another piece he couldn't make fit into the puzzle of Harmony Duprie. Why would she drive a beat-up old Pinto when she had money to spend on expensive books?

Jake hadn't eaten lunch, or breakfast, and the Pink Flamingo seemed as good of a place as any to grab a bite. Maybe he'd get lucky and the cute waitress would serve him. She'd be fun to flirt with, and he suspected she'd be happy to flirt back. He'd have to stop there. If Duprie caught wind of anything beyond that, it would destroy his chances with her, and end his plot for getting his hands on the book.

As if summoned by his thoughts, there she stood by the restaurant entrance, talking to an old lady. What had changed from her normal schedule? He pulled into the farthest parking space because he didn't want her to spot him. Not yet. He leaned over, checked his reflection in the rear-view mirror, and swept his hand across his dark-brown hair. It was time for a trim, but Duprie might be one of those women who liked to run their fingers through a man's hair. He'd wait.

A second old lady exited the restaurant, then another. Duprie held the door for each of them. When a fourth came out, he jumped out of the car, jogged to the entrance, and seized the opportunity. Jake couldn't tell if Duprie was coming or going, but her good manners had her acting as a doorman, and he'd earn points by taking over her duties. He didn't have to fake the grin that lit his face as he winked at her and reached for the door handle.

Their hands touched for the barest moment, but he didn't push it by letting the contact stretch out. It was like taming a wild horse. She'd bolt if he moved too fast. He half-bowed and swept his free hand to indicate her freedom. A slight red color highlighted her cheeks as she hurried inside.

Another old lady came out while he watched. The waitress—not the cute one—led Duprie to a booth. Jake wondered how she'd react if he joined her. That would push things too fast and too soon. He closed the door and returned to his car to seek a different place for supper. He'd wait to make his move.

# Chapter 2

Pity he wasn't a pickpocket. The historical house known as Fallingwater had sounded like the perfect setup for a heist, but after surveying the grounds, Jake wasn't so sure. He pretended to admire the pale-pink springtime foliage and the building in the distance, but it was the people in line that drew his attention as he studied them for possibilities and wondered if the lines were always this long. Crowds cramped his style.

"Your wife drag you here, too?" asked the overweight middle-aged man in line behind him. The lady by his side frowned and rolled her eyes.

"Worse." Jake grimaced. He had no desire to make a temporary friend but leads for jobs came from unexpected places. "This was supposed to be our first date, and she canceled on me. Since I'd already bought the tickets and was halfway here, I came anyway." He shrugged. "I'm a glutton for punishment."

"Oh, you'll enjoy it," the lady said. "I'm Dal, and this is Sam." She ran her hand through her short, bleached-blonde hair. "This is our third trip here. I'm trying to come once each season, and this is the first time I've seen the rhododendrons in full bloom. I can't wait to see the inside of the house because the sunlight in the interior changes as the seasons do. With the clear skies, it should be spectacular!"

The day was looking up. With a built-in tour guide like Dal, Jake would get the details the normal tour guides glossed over. Plus, he'd spotted a lady with a large diamond ring on her right hand. It would take no work at all to liberate the diamond from the prongs holding it in place. Shoot, if she noticed it missing, he'd join the crowd looking for it. The diamond wouldn't be worth much at a pawnshop, but the thrill was the real payoff.

Walking up the narrow stairway to the second floor, Jake became convinced the ample rear of the diamond lady was a marvel of modern technology. It didn't sway nearly as much as it should have as she struggled up the steps.

The moment happened with no help from Jake. Diamond lady tripped on the lace of her heeled sandals and tumbled to the concrete stairs.

"Are you okay?" Jake placed one hand on the small of her back and the other on her shoulder.

She pushed herself off the stairs and, with a little sob, clung to Jake's arm. Dal offered a tissue, and between steadying the lady, wiping the dirt from her hands, and helping her the rest of the way up the stairs, it was a done deal.

By the time the tour was over, and he'd spent ample time wandering the grounds, Jake was more cheerful than he'd been in days. The diamond was tucked into the slit in the hem of his pants. He'd spotted at least one flaw in the security setup of the exhibit hall. Dal and Sam had insisted on buying him lunch at the overpriced museum cafeteria. Plus, he'd gotten the number of one of the female employees. It would only take a couple of dates to get her to reveal the employee entrance. Yes, things were looking good.

❋ ❋ ❋

Things looked even better from the second-floor balcony of the Oak Grove Library as Jake watched Duprie hustle around on the first floor, putting books away and talking to the library's customers—no, patrons. He needed to attract her attention. What could he ask to get more than a simple yes or no answer? He had never spent much time in libraries even when he was in school, ages ago. He'd have to rely on instinct.

Jake spotted his opportunity when she picked up a large stack of magazines and opened one to read as she strolled towards the other side of the library. he grabbed a random book off the shelf and sneaked down the stairs. He didn't want her to hear him coming.

As she turned a corner, he walked in front of her, pretending to read his book. His timing was perfect. She ran right into him. The magazines tumbled to the floor. Her brown eyes, magnified by her thick glasses, were cartoonishly large.

"I'm sorry," she said as she knelt to retrieve the magazines. "I have a bad habit of not watching where I'm going."

Jake, chuckling, knelt on the floor to assist her. The pink in her cheeks revealed her embarrassment, and he wasn't above using that to his advantage. The way the magazines had fallen, it was easy to make sure their arms bumped as he helped pick them up. As he handed her his share of the loot, the pink turned to a deep red.

When she stood, she almost lost her balance. With his swift reflexes, he was able to grab her arm and hold her steady. Her eyes got even bigger as he leaned in. "It seems Fate has decreed that we meet. Third time's a charm and all that. I'm Jake Hennessey. And I'd offer to shake your hand but I'm afraid you'll drop those magazines again."

The blush spread, but she recovered her manners and held out her hand. "I'm Harmony Duprie, the research librarian. Thank you for your help, Mr. Hennessey."

"Just the person I need! Do you have any books about the history of the old houses in Oak Grove? Victorian era?" The question came out of nowhere, but based on the way her eyes lit up, he'd found the right button to push. Jake felt guilty for taking advantage of her naivete but holding the cash in his hands after he sold the book would wash away the guilt.

"We only have one. You have to use it in the library."

"That'll be fine."

"I'll show you where we keep it. But if you don't

mind, I need to put these away first." She bounced the magazines in her arms.

Jake reached out, afraid she'd drop them again. "Perhaps I can help you. That way the job will go faster."

They spent the next five minutes putting the magazines in their places. With the information he'd gathered from the library in Pittsburgh, Jake knew enough to sort them by date. After watching her straighten each stack of magazines, he did the same. It earned him points—it showed in the way she kept checking out how he was doing.

The need to whisper made it hard to flirt, putting him at a disadvantage. He pretended to show interest in several of the business magazines, but that was as far as he took it. When they finished the job, she led him to a musty, small room. Shelves holding books with faded and tattered covers lined one wall.

"A historical group released this book back in the 40s," she said, removing an oversized gray volume from the shelf. "I know a few families have copies in their personal collections, but this is the only one the public has access to, so please be careful with it." She placed it on a small table in the center of the room.

"The library kept it all these years?" Jake asked.

To his surprise, a hint of red blossomed in her cheeks. "No, it came from a local pawnshop a few years ago and was donated to the library."

Why would that make her blush? Unless she was the one who ran across it. He flipped through the first few pages to see if there was a notation of where it came from. Not finding one, he tucked the information into his memory to retrieve if it was needed later.

He spent an hour scanning the book. Duprie would wander by every so often, but he pretended not to notice. He was wary of coming on too strong or too fast. She'd never make the first move and he had to plan his with care. Supper sounded like a good idea. Leave without saying goodbye, return later and spring the invite on the unsuspecting lady. Jake would have her right where he wanted her.

✳ ✳ ✳

Flowers would be too much. Jake suspected she'd like them, but he'd hold off for now. From across the street, he studied the flow of patrons in and out of the library. If he asked her out in front of witnesses, would it be harder for her to refuse? Too much of his plan was riding on this, and he had a moment of doubt. Ripping off a spoiled rich girl was one thing, but she didn't fit that category.

But a job was a job. And this one held the promise of a rich reward. He straightened the sleeves of his suit coat and climbed the steps that led to the library. He'd scouted out the wheelchair ramp in the back, and the employee entrance in the basement, but wanted to make a grand entrance if she happened to be watching.

Which she wasn't. She sat at the front desk with several piles of books hiding her face. A short line of people waited for her attention, and he took his place at the end of it.

When it was his turn, he plastered on his best smile and waited for her to look up.

"Oh! Mr. Hennessey!" She blinked rapidly as if trying to focus. "Is there something I can help you with? Another book? You'll have to apply for a card if you want to take anything out of the library."

She was rambling, showing her nervousness. That evened the score.

Jake grinned. "You can help me, but not with a book. I'm in need of a companion for dinner, and I wonder if you would accompany me? When you get off work, of course." He regretted the way the words came out. He'd over-planned and messed up.

Duprie frowned. "Sorry, but the 1930s called. They miss you and want you to go home."

So, the lady had a sharp tongue under that quiet exterior. This could be fun. Jake allowed his grin to grow. "I got carried away. Blame it on anxiousness. Let's try this again. How about supper? My treat?"

She hesitated long enough to worry Jake. "What time?"

"Six?" Jake's internal smile matched his exterior one. "You pick a place. I'm not familiar with Oak Grove's restaurants." Although he'd checked out a few of its less-reputable bars.

"Do you like Italian?" she asked, after a moment's thought.

He lifted an eyebrow. "You wouldn't be referring to Mama D's, would you? I stumbled across it a few nights ago and can't wait to go back." That was the truth. It offered big-city quality Italian food at small-town prices.

"I'll meet you there," she said.

Jake had wanted to pick her up at her place. That would have given him an opening to walk her up her stairs and maybe farther. But he'd play by her rules for the moment. He didn't allow his smile to slip. "See you there."



A fifty—part of the proceeds from the sale of the diamond—ensured the best booth and the best server at Mama D's. Jake probably could have gotten by with less. He had the impression Mama D herself had a soft spot for Duprie, but, struck by the urge to make the night magic, he opted to make a big splash.

She arrived promptly at six. With a genuine smile, Jake rose to greet her. She'd switched out of her dull-gray business suit into a simple deep-blue dress that sparkled in the light as she moved. If he could talk her into wearing contacts and changing her hairstyle, she'd be absolutely stunning.

He caught himself before the thought went any farther. *She was a job*, he reminded himself. *Get the book and disappear. No long-term relationships allowed.*



"I never understood why the band kids and the art kids didn't get along." Jake finished what was left of his glass of red wine. "It seems to me they were all creative, just headed down different paths."

They'd wandered into the topic from a discussion about the homeschooled kids that Harmony dealt with regularly. Jake couldn't put a finger on the exact moment she'd moved from being Duprie to Harmony in his head, but he'd fight with himself about it later. He was too busy enjoying the conversation and the company.

She took a sip of her iced tea. "Which one were you?"

He'd never tell her the truth. But what subject could he claim that wouldn't trip him up? "Neither. I was into archeology." He leaned forward and put his hand on top of hers. "Were you part of the creative writing group?"

Her laughter sparkled. "Heavens, no. I was a history fanatic. That's where I found my love of old houses."

That was his perfect in, but she didn't give him the chance to use it.

"They're getting ready to close." She tilted her head towards a waitress filling salt and pepper shakers. "We need to leave."

Jake wasn't ready for the night to end. Harmony had been surprisingly good company. Witty and smart, not what he'd expected from a small-town librarian. He unwillingly let go of her hand and stood. "I guess we should get out of their way."

"You pay at the register up front," she said as she followed his lead and pushed her chair away from the table. "I'm going to make a quick trip to the restroom, and I'll meet you there."

It would give him time to regain his mental balance. Something about her threw him off. That was dangerous. He nodded. "I'll be waiting!"

The brief delay after he paid was worth it to see her

coming in his direction with a shy smile on her face. The blue dress clung to her in all the right places, and for a moment, he regretted his career choice. "Did I tell you how beautiful you are?" he asked when she reached him. He loved making her blush.

Harmony hit him lightly on the shoulder. "You're such a flatterer."

All in the game, Jake thought. But she made it easy. "You deserve someone to flatter you every day. Can I walk you to your car?" He held the door open for her.

She pointed across the street. "It's right over there."

"The little red one?" he asked, although he knew better.

She giggled. "No, the blue Pinto. His name is George."

Jake stopped in the middle of the street. "George?" He waited for two heartbeats. "There's a story behind that I'd love to hear." A car coming their direction forced them to hurry the rest of the way. "But not tonight. If I ask you to come to my hotel, you'll turn me down and that would hurt my ego."

They reached the car, and Jake waited while Harmony dug through her purse, looking for her keys.

"Thanks for supper," she said. "I had a great time."

So had Jake. "Can I call you the next time I'm in town?" He half-expected her to turn him down, but she rattled off her number. He pretended to not get it the first time around, so she had to repeat it. After entering it in his contacts, he dialed it immediately. "This way you'll answer it and not think it's a spammer," he said, grinning.

From the depths of her purse came a melody he almost recognized. It came to him just before she answered.

"Hello," she said, smiling at him.

"Goodbye," Jake replied, and hung up the call. "John Denver? That's another story you need to tell me."

Harmony tucked her phone back into her purse. "But not tonight."

He nodded. "Not tonight. I should be back in a couple of weeks. I'll hold you to your promise then."

She unlocked her car. "Thanks again," she said.

"How about a goodnight kiss?" What was he doing? That wasn't part of the plan. But he couldn't back out now.

She lifted her chin and stared into Jake's eyes. He had to keep this light. He leaned in and barely touched his lips to hers before pulling away.

It wasn't enough. Not letting her change her mind, Jake mashed his mouth against hers. He ran his tongue over her lips and pushed his body against hers. His arm wrapped around her waist, tugging her closer, and she melted into his embrace. It still wasn't enough. A car horn blared, and she pulled away.

She reached up and touched his cheek. "Good night, Jake."

He'd been dismissed. He wanted more but took the hint and held the door open while she climbed in and fastened her seatbelt. With one hand on the door, he bent over and kissed her forehead. "Good night, Angel," he said, before straightening and closing the door.

He was in so much trouble.

# Chapter 3

To Jake's practiced eye, the jewelry displays at the pawnshop near the motel needed additional items. He wondered if the store was strapped for cash. He was there to sell a silver ring he'd 'found' on the street, and worried he wouldn't get the price he wanted.

At least he'd already sent Duprie a gift: an expensive bouquet that the saleslady assured him was correct for the occasion. Something about the language of flowers and pink camellias.

That had been a week ago. The time and distance had eased his guilt. It was back to business as usual.

And old man with several teeth missing shuffled out of the back room. "Can I help you?"

"You guys shutting down?" Jake asked. He waved a hand towards the case. "It's a little bare."

"Naw," the clerk answered. "The owner got word of a string of robberies from shops in the city. He's taking precautions."

Not a good place for Jake to be. He didn't want to work in the same area as another professional and somehow get tied into their quest. Or interfere with it. But he was too close to success to pull out now.

"I thought you guys had all kinds of hidden security cameras."

"We do. But he's in disguise—wears masks of people in that space show that's so popular—and he's coming in, smashing the case, grabbing what he can, and running."

Jake knew of only one person who worked like that, a man by the name of Ben who operated on the west coast. They'd run into each other a couple of times, and Jake had pulled him out of a bad setup once, saving his hide. It never hurt to have someone owe him a favor.

"Well, be careful." *Back to business.* "How much can you give me for this ring?"

The ten bucks Jake tucked into his wallet was more than he expected. The money would come in handy, but his actual goal had been to scope out the shop and see how open they were to buying items under the table. He was always looking for new markets. First impressions told Jake this one operated strictly by the law and wouldn't be of any use to him.

Next on his list was finding a different motel. He had a rule about not staying in the same place for very long. Despite taking the waitress from the museum out for supper, he hadn't gotten any new leads about the jewelry exhibit. He was bored and figured he'd waited long enough to make his next move on Duprie.

It was an excuse to see her again. But it was Wednesday, her night out with friends. He'd hold off, hit up a bar and make some more acquaintances instead. Not friends. There were rules to follow. Don't get too close to anyone.

* * *

He double-checked that he didn't smell like weed. If he'd known the bar suggested by the motel's front desk clerk was a cop hangout, he would have gone somewhere else. But the beer was cold and cheap and as long as he sat in a corner and didn't stick his nose where it wasn't wanted, he'd be okay. His chances of picking up a woman were slim, because every one he eyed was either flirting with a cop or was an officer herself. But, by eavesdropping, he might learn a thing or two.

Except these cops were more interested in the baseball game on TV than talking shop. Not a word about the pawnshop break-ins. It was early in the season, but they were already betting on how far the Pirates would go. Jake didn't know enough about the team to join in the friendly banter, so he pretended to read the newspaper another customer left behind. He limited himself to two beers before heading back to the motel. It wasn't as nice as the last one, so he'd switch again in a few days. Or he'd rent a room in Oak Grove itself to be closer to Duprie on the off chance she'd agree to spend the night with him.

He shouldn't be thinking like that. She was strictly business.

*  *  *

As he sat in his car across the street from the library, waiting for her to get off work, he knew better.

He waited to make his move, watching her as she walked down the stairs, not paying attention to anything around her. Anyone could have rushed up to her, grabbed her purse, and she'd never catch up to them. It was good that she lived in a small town where that sort of thing didn't happen. He'd have to teach her how to protect herself.

There were lots of things he wanted to teach her. If he delayed stealing the book, he could do that. Or figure out a way to grab it and point the evidence at someone else. The challenge would stretch his skills, but he'd look like a hero in the end.

He was right behind her when she fumbled with her purse, looking for her keys, but she wasn't aware of his presence. She unlocked her car, climbed in, and fastened her seatbelt without ever seeing him. When she went to close her door, he put his hand on the top of the frame so it wouldn't swing shut.

She looked annoyed and tried again. It didn't work. Jake didn't hide the grin that creased his face. She finally glanced up and saw him. The smile that lit her face sealed his doom.

"Jake! I didn't know you were in town."

"I have a meeting in Pittsburgh tomorrow afternoon. I thought I'd come early to see you." He offered his hand to help her out of the car, which left them standing close enough together that he could count the individual pieces in her turquoise necklace.

A wrinkle formed in her forehead. "You won't get in trouble with your boss, will you?"

How long would he be able to maintain the lie that he worked for a construction firm? "As long as I make it on time, he won't care. Can I take you out for supper? Someplace easy so you don't have to go home and change? That way we'll have more time together."

"You're going to spoil me," she laughed. "By the way, thank you for the flowers. You made my co-workers jealous."

The Dairy Barn felt like a blast from the 60s, a teenage hangout from a TV show. Faded red vinyl on the seats of the booths, servers in short-sleeve shirts with white collars, and a jukebox in the corner. Jake imagined it playing music from Woodstock instead of recent pop songs. He speculated about the amount of cash the staff kept in their pockets. Easy enough to bump into one of them and walk away with a handful of small bills, mostly ones, but he didn't work that way.

He hadn't counted on Harmony being so popular. He'd been told countless times that he was attractive and garnered the stares to give some validity to the idea, but it wasn't like the attention she received. Half of the customers and most of the staff stopped by the booth to tell her hi or ask her a question about the library. She was polite to all of them, but Jake read the telltale signs she would prefer to be left alone. It felt like hanging out with a local rock star.

"Ready to go?" he asked, putting his half-eaten

burger on his plate. Harmony had only finished a third of hers.

She blew out a deep breath. "I'm sorry. I didn't think they'd be this busy."

"Not your fault. We can ask for doggy bags and go sit in the park to eat. Or go to your place."

She bit her bottom lip. "I'll need to go back to the car and grab a sweater."

Jake didn't remember if there was a blanket in the rental car and he'd left his jacket at the motel, but she'd ignored his suggestion about stopping by her apartment and he wasn't going to push her, as much as he wanted to. "We could go park somewhere and keep the heater running."

"There's the Point. I haven't been there for years." Harmony giggled. "It's the teenagers' make-out spot. It's a little place on a hill above town."

Heat flared in Jake's veins. He raised a hand to get their waitress' attention. "Can we get the bill and to-go bags?" he asked when she came over.

The waitress didn't seem fazed by the request. When she returned, she brought along two large foam cups in a holder. "Harmony always gets a chocolate shake for dessert. I didn't know if she planned on sharing, so I brought you one, too, for free. I noticed y'all were getting interrupted the whole time and didn't enjoy your meal."

Harmony stuck a straw into each lid. "That's so sweet, Sally. Thank you."

"Enjoy the rest of your night." Sally leaned down and whispered something in Harmony's ear. Jake strained to hear it, but only caught bits and pieces, not entire words.

He waited until they were outside to ask about it.

"You have a lot of friends," he said as they strolled to the car. He wanted to wrap his arm around her waist, but he was carrying the leftovers.

Harmony shook her head. "What I have is a bunch of older folks who think I still need to be looked after. When my parents died, half the town pitched in to help me get through it."

Another story he needed to hear, but not this night, unless she wanted to share. He stayed quiet and let her take the lead.

"Do you like astronomy?" she asked as they reached the car.

It took him a minute to catch up to the abrupt change of subject. "Not really. I grew up in a big city, and the streetlights wash out the stars. I might find the Big Dipper but that's the limit of my experience." He unlocked the car and opened the passenger side door for her.

She waited until he climbed into the driver's seat to continue the conversation. "Then you're in for a treat. There are only a few clouds, and the Point is a great place for star-watching. I can show you how to find the North Star. Start slow."

There were a few things he wanted to teach her. But not in a car. Doing it right required a bed. Or at least a soft surface where they could move with ease. "Sounds like a plan."


It was just a dirt parking lot at the top of a large hill, but it had a sweeping view of Oak Grove spreading below it. Two other cars were there, but both left shortly after Jake and Harmony arrived.

It was still warm enough to lean against the hood of the car to finish their supper and not worry about jackets. Jake didn't remember the last time he'd been on a picnic. Probably a school field trip. His mother didn't have time for such activities when he was a kid. There'd been many days when he had to eat dry, cold cereal or nothing at all for supper while she was out drinking. When he got older, he'd figured out how to wrangle supper invites from friends or his Aunt Tillie.

They ate to the songs sung by birds and crickets. When he finished, he crumbled up his burger wrapper and stuffed it in the bag, then held it open so Harmony could do the same. To his surprise, she took the bag from him.

"While we're at it," she said. "We might as well pick up some of the trash other people have left."

"Won't the wind blow it away?" There wasn't much garbage anyway, not that he spotted with a quick glance.

"That doesn't make it any better. Then it messes up the woods. You don't litter, do you?"

He had the feeling the answer was a game-changer. He answered with care. "Nope. I believe in leaving no trace behind." *For other reasons than a clean environment.* "I don't smoke, either." A small white lie. He didn't smoke tobacco.

She picked up a fast-food wrapper and put it in the bag. He didn't see any way to get around it without offending her, so he joined in the hunt. The small bag wouldn't take long to fill.

By the time they finished the chore, the sun had set, and a chill crept into the air. Another car parked on the opposite side of the lot and it made Jake uncomfortable, as if he'd been caught doing something illegal. Which was laughable, because that was part of his life.

He put the garbage on the floorboard of the back seat, then stood by Harmony. "So, how do we find the North Star?"

"It isn't dark enough yet. But you can look for the evening star and make a wish."

"The evening star? What's that?"

She shot a sharp glance in his direction. "Really? You don't know?"

He didn't have to pretend and shrugged. "Nope."

"Star light, star bright?" She raised an eyebrow in question. "The planet Venus?"

"What are you talking about?"

She turned to face him and grasped his hands. "Star light, star bright, the first star I see tonight? Didn't you ever wish upon a star?"

He shook his head, pulled her closer, and stared into her eyes. "No. What's it do?"

"If you wish upon the first star you see, your wish is supposed to come true. But you can't tell anyone what it was."

"I've made my wish," he said in a husky voice. "But only you can make it come true."

The line should have worked. It had worked for him before.

But Harmony laughed and let go of his hands. "You're slick. That sounds like it's ripped from the pages of a romance novel. Didn't think you were the kind of guy who read books to get hints on what to say to women."

She'd hurt his ego, but he'd never admit it. "Do I get points for trying?"

"Two," she replied promptly. "Two out of five." Then she turned her back to him and, with a grand sweep of her right arm, pointed to the horizon where a sliver of light remained. "See the brightest star? That's Venus, the planet, also the evening star. Turns out she's the morning star, too."

Jake put his hands on her shoulders and stood close enough to nuzzle her neck. "Isn't Venus the goddess of love?"

"Yes."

"And how do I make a wish?" He kissed her ear.

"Star light, star bright," she said, with a hitch in her voice.

"Star light, star bright," he repeated.

# Chapter 4

"I wish I may, I wish I might," Jake muttered on the drive back to his motel. The stars weren't aligning, no matter how hard he tried. He was no closer to securing an invitation to Harmony's apartment.

Several carloads of teenagers arriving just as things were getting interesting had ruined the mood and his hopes of persuading her to take a chance on him. But the kiss they'd exchanged when he dropped her off at her car still burned in his veins. He needed a drink and a cold shower, in no particular order.

He'd gotten too close to her, and the hurt he would cause by stealing the book weighed on what little soul he had left. It was time to disappear for a few weeks and rethink the job. She wasn't what he had expected and presented an ongoing challenge. He liked that. Hell, he liked her.

At the package store where he stopped to buy a fifth of his second-favorite whiskey, he picked up a copy of Plain Dealer, Cleveland's newspaper. He didn't care about the news, he could get that from the TV.

The society pages revealed who had recently worn an interesting piece of jewelry to a wedding or other event, and perhaps not returned it to their safe deposit box. Experience had taught him that high-end items were put back in a day or two. Ones that weren't worth as much might stay in the owner's home for a month. That made them easier to acquire.

He'd removed Pittsburgh from his list of targets. With the pawnshop burglar active, people would be more careful with their jewels. Besides, he didn't want to interfere with another professional's setup.

The wedding of the Raetners' grandson and the Groots' daughter seemed like the perfect opportunity. He wouldn't touch the newlyweds or the wedding party, but the guests provided him with multiple possibilities. Anything to get his mind off Harmony Duprie.

❉ ❉ ❉

Jake studied his reflection in the mirror. The black hair dye would wash out with a couple of showers. The deep brown makeup he'd applied below his cheekbones cast the illusion of a narrow face. He settled a pair of heavy-rimmed glasses low on his nose as a finishing touch.

The venue by the lake promised the ultimate wedding experience for the happy couple. Azaleas and camellias blooming everywhere, soft breezes coming off the water, a subtle fragrance of roses wafting in the air. The open bar was an added amenity that worked in Jake's favor.

He'd hit up the hotel's bar last night in a reconnaissance mission and made the acquaintance of an off-duty member of the banquet staff. Well, officially off the clock. Kent, a mid-twenties surfer-type, had been promised free drinks, double-time, and a room if he stayed after-hours and covered room service.

"Tomorrow's going to be a real pain," he'd complained, sipping his third glass of wine. "Half the guys caught the bug that's going around. I guess it's a spring flu. Anyway, the boss had to hire help from a temp agency for tomorrow."

Just the way in Jake needed. He'd attach himself to an unsuspecting and inexperienced fill-in to gain access to the banquet hall. After that, crashing the wedding would be easy. All he had to do was look and act like he belonged. He refilled Kent's glass from the carafe on the table. "What's happening tomorrow?"

"Big wedding. They expect 500 guests. At least we aren't doing a sit-down service. That would be a disaster. Hey, you aren't here for it, are you?"

"Not me. I planned to meet a buddy here, but his wife made him stay home."

"Bummer."

"Hey, Kent, you're up," the bartender called. "Order for 2213."

Kent stood. "If you're sticking around, save my seat for me, will ya'? There's a free drink in it for you."

Jake straightened his tie. Would his disguise be enough to fool Kent? Of course, as drunk as Kent had been by the end of the night, he probably wouldn't remember Jake. The opening strains of the small orchestra warming up was his warning that the party was about to begin. He stashed the duffel bag with his spare clothes in an empty locker and, with a mix of anticipation and foreboding, tugged on the sleeves of his tailored suit coat to straighten them, then stepped out into the hall.

"Ready for a refill, Derek?" Jake asked the skinny blond he'd spotted sipping from a pocket flask during the ceremony. The name came courtesy of the man's mother ordering him to get her a drink.

"It's the only way to make it through one of these events," Derek said. He peered at Jake. "Do I know you?"

"Jake Hennessey. We met at your cousin's wedding five years ago." He'd overheard some guests comparing the two events.

Derek blinked. "Sure. Now I remember. You have a restaurant or something, right?"

Jake could work with that. "Close. It's a franchise of an Italian chain." He smiled. "I have three locations. You promised to come by but never did."

"Sorry about that." Derek put his hand on Jake's shoulder. "Let me get you a drink."

That's all it took. With Derek at his side, Jake made the rounds, mingling with the relatives and sizing up potential targets. As long as he kept Derek drunk enough to be annoying but not angry, everyone was happy to allow Jake to babysit him. That meant no one questioned who Jake was or why he was at the wedding.

It was a science that Jake had mastered. The bartenders quickly caught on to Jake's strategy and played along. Only every third drink was full strength, and most of them were left sitting on an empty table halfway through.

He scanned the area while waiting for the next round. Still no sign of Kent. Good. Even better, Derek had fastened his attention on a gray-haired lady wearing a brooch that glittered in the sunlight. Just the person Jake wanted to meet.

"Here's a fresh drink, Derek," he said, holding it out. "Don't lose this one. The bartender was giving me the evil eye." Not even close to the truth. He'd convinced Derek that he needed to pay his non-existent bill with the bar. Jake had taken half the money and given the other half to the bartenders as a rather large tip.

Derek shook his head. "I get so busy visiting. Like, Aunt Edith was telling me about a rock concert they have each year."

Edith raised an eyebrow. "Jazz," she said. "It's a jazz festival."

Jake caught her eye and winked. "I know nothing about music, but even I don't get the two mixed up." He offered his hand. "I don't think we've met, have we? Edith, is it?"

She accepted his hand, and Jake let his fingers stroke her inner wrist. "Edith Bargen," she said, the color rising in her cheeks. "You are?"

Derek rushed to answer. "My friend, Jake

Harrigan." Derek had somehow swapped the last name earlier, and Jake hadn't corrected him. "He owns a chain of restaurants."

"Any in the Provinceville area?" Edith asked.

Jake shook his head. "I don't believe so. Where is Provinceville?"

"Massachusetts. Cape Cod area. It's a small town, but the scenery is amazing."

While she rambled on, Jake studied the brooch above her left breast and made mutters of agreement at appropriate times. Those were genuine diamonds, but he couldn't spot a way to make it his own. Not unless she had a medical emergency and Jake couldn't count on that happening, not with her being in apparently good shape despite her age.

"I'll have to play tourist and visit someday." Or pretend to be a tourist when he had another goal in mind. "When's the best time to come?" What he really hoped for was information on when Edith wouldn't be home.

But Derek had finished his drink and was getting fidgety. He put a hand on Jake's shoulder. "Hey, there's Vaughn." With his other hand, he waved in the direction of the food tables. "You really need to meet this guy. It's been great chatting with you, Aunt Edith."

"With Marducci as quarterback, I think the Browns have a chance," Vaughn said. "They've had a great preseason performance."

"No way," Derek snorted. "Not as long as Barakat

and Janes are on defense. Those guys can't stop a wet noodle."

Jake hovered near the small group of men, pretending to care about the discussion, but actually eying the gold and ruby tie tack Vaughn wore, and waiting for the right moment. He knew the perfect new home for it.

"As long as Barakat doesn't get injured this year, he'll do fine." Vaughn took a sip from his glass of fortified iced tea. Jake had caught him adding a hefty dose of rum to it.

"He gets hurt every year. What makes you think this year will be any different?" Derek threw one arm up in the air—the one holding his drink. What was left in the glass sloshed out and splattered on three of the men, most of it hitting Vaughn.

It was Jake's moment to shine. He grabbed a napkin from a nearby table and tossed it to Vaughn, but it dropped short. They bumped as they both reached to grab it from the floor, and when they stood, the napkin was in Vaughn's hand, but the tie tack was in Jake's pocket.

Vaughn dabbed at the moisture on his tuxedo jacket. "Thanks a lot, asshole."

"Sorry," Derek said with a half-hearted grin.

Jake grabbed Derek's arm. "I think we need to go for a walk," he said. "Clear your head. Go smell the roses or something." He jerked his chin towards Vaughn before leaving. "Nice meeting you."

By the end of the party, he ended up with an

unneeded invitation to join Derek at an after-hours bar, several hundred dollars in his wallet, a silver ring in his shoe and a high-quality pearl necklace in his interior jacket pocket. Not heritage jewelry, but not bought in the last two years, either. All it took was offering to help the lady in question slip on her sweater when a chilly breeze blew in off the lake and it didn't matter if he broke the thin chain. The gold would get melted down for scrap at one pawnshop and the pearls sold individually at several others. And, of course, the tie tack. Not a big take, but it scratched the itch. Not bad for a day's work.

As he drove away from the venue, he headed west towards Chicago and his favorite fence. He liked to give her first shot at the good stuff. If he got lucky, she'd be so pleased with his take, she'd welcome him to her bed. No commitment, no attachment. It was safer that way. Maybe she'd chase Harmony out of his system.

❋ ❋ ❋

"Have you heard the rumors about the smash-and-grab expert moving to the Pittsburgh area?" he asked while Ruby scrambled up some eggs for breakfast. That's why he'd wanted the tie tack. She loved the way the rubies looked against her copper-colored skin. Ruby had a collection of her namesake jewels and adding to it put her in the mood to give him a better price for his goods. "You need to be careful."

"We're on alert. The story I got is that he's a copycat. But good." Ruby flipped the eggs. "How d'you hear about him?"

"I'm doing research in the area. Backed off. He's attracting too many cops and making things dangerous."

"Or she. How much salt and pepper you want? There's one theory that the thief is female."

It was possible, although most women in the business didn't have the strength for that kind of work. "You make the best eggs. You decide. So, you think that he or she is a competitor?"

She divided the eggs between two plates. "It's possible. Or a druggie looking for a quick buck. No worries, if they head this way, I'll be ready. Come, eat."

He sat at the small table in the pocket kitchen. Ruby hid her money well. From looking at her place, no one would guess her bank balance. Jake had seen it once, when he examined her statement while she slept after a vigorous session in bed.

"Be careful. I worry about you," he said before taking his first bite.

She snorted. "Me? I'm good." She tapped the spot under her left arm where she carried her revolver. "But are you sure I can't sell you a piece? You're the one working alone."

"I appreciate the offer, but you know my rule. No guns. I can't stop the bad guys from shooting at me, but the cops won't see me as a threat."

Ruby grinned. "Do I need to remind you that you're one of the bad guys?"

He didn't feel that way. It was a game to him. He wasn't the best player, but he was good, and working to get better. If he pulled off the heist from Duprie, it would move him up to very good.

He ditched the car at the Chicago branch of the rental company, where he caught a shuttle to O'Hare airport. He paid cash for the ticket to Atlanta, plus meals and a postcard. Jake hated having to use his actual name to clear security, but at least there wasn't a credit card record of the purchases.

Nothing waited for him at the end of the plane ride but a dingy studio apartment and the possibility of a job working as a bouncer. That and his souped-up Dodge Charger, his prized possession. The occasional jobs at several local bars kept him legitimate in the eyes of the government and less of a target for law enforcement. He didn't know how long he'd stay this time.

Or he could make a stop in Pittsburgh. Drive to Oak Grove and visit Duprie. She was stuck in his head. He couldn't decide which he wanted more. To snatch the book or to make love to her. Over and over again.

The other option was a trip to Provinceville, Massachusetts. A diamond brooch waited for him there.

❄ ❄ ❄

Tiny place as towns go, but all the tourists in Provinceville made it easier to hide in. Jake bleached his hair and wore lifts to alter his appearance. It was the wardrobe change that made the biggest difference. The shorts, straw hat, and jazz band t-shirts would be discarded at the end of the trip. He hoped the three weeks he'd spent assembling the wardrobe and doing his research would pay off.

The Bargen house was simple to break into. It was

well-maintained, but Jake knew the tricks. The windows were the easiest point of entry once the family left to go to a concert. With the police busy controlling the crowds, the neighborhoods were unguarded.

The locked doors would be easy to pick, but that left behind traces a good cop would find. The first window Jake tried was firmly latched, and he didn't want to break a window if he didn't need to. But they'd left the kitchen window open a crack. He had to go through at an angle to get his shoulders through the narrow opening and use his arms to pull the rest of his body past the sink and onto the floor.

He waited a few seconds for his eyes to adjust to the semi-darkness. Older people favored nightlights throughout their house. They gave him all the light he needed to work. There hadn't been time to scope out the interior, so he crept from room to room to find the main bedroom.

The door stood open, but he slipped on the latex gloves he'd swiped from the motel before he entered. If he got lucky, the case and the brooch would be sitting on top of the dresser. He hoped Mrs. Bargen hadn't worn it. But the cluttered tray held no jewelry box.

He worked quickly, opening and closing each drawer, not finding what he was looking for. The next place to check was the closet. He turned on the light and closed the door behind him. And hit paydirt.

The back of the closet was lined with shelves. Among the sweaters and flowered scarves, Jake spotted numerous boxes bearing the names of prominent jewelers. If Edith kept Cartier and Dior pieces in her house, what did she have in her safe-deposit box? He'd love to get his hands on a Belperron. But that wasn't why he was here.

A small, unmarked box tucked under the lingerie caught Jake's attention. He opened the box with care, in case the contents were loose. When he saw what it contained, he didn't know whether to be disappointed or exhilarated.

It wasn't the diamond brooch, but it contained a pair of exquisite white gold, diamond, and jade drop earrings. They had to be worth twice as much as the brooch, and it would be a crime to have them melted down to sell off the stones. He wondered if Edith had planned to wear them but changed her mind.

A dealer in Savannah would buy them as they were. He slipped the earrings out of the box and into the hidden compartment in his belt. Then he returned the box to the shelf but pushed it farther back. Unless she checked it, it would be a long time before Edith noticed anything missing.

After turning off the overhead light, Jake waited for his eyes to adjust. He cracked open the closet door to make sure the house remained quiet. The faint sounds of the concert reached his ears, so he still had time to make a clean exit.

In the darkened house, he glided down the stairs and to the kitchen. There, he lowered the window to its original position, straightened up the dishes he'd disturbed, and used the dishcloth to wipe away any prints. Like he owned the place, he strolled out the back door, locking the door behind him.

The walk to the concert grounds was timed perfectly

with the end of the performance. He joined the tired but excited crowd headed to the harbor and the ferry. The motel in Boston waited.

He'd bought a postcard during his time in Boston, but it joined the one from Chicago in his cupboard. Until he'd been officially invited to Harmony's apartment, he'd pretend he didn't know where she lived. Another trip to Pittsburgh had to wait until he met his contact in Savannah to pass off the earrings. They hadn't sold for as much as he wanted, but he didn't want to take the risk of holding onto them long enough to up the price.

# Chapter 5

Stuck behind two semi-trucks driving side by side down the road, Jake beat on the steering wheel. He'd brought his own car and hoped to reach Oak Grove in time to catch Harmony leaving work. But between the pelting summer thunderstorm and the traffic jam in Pittsburgh, he'd already missed his chance.

The reservation for the motel at the Oak Grove exit ensured he wouldn't end up spending the night in a parking lot. It was past suppertime on a Thursday, and he expected traffic to lighten as people reached their destinations. Duprie would be home, tucked into her apartment, and he wouldn't have to worry about running into her barhopping. Of course, he'd visit establishments she'd never set foot in. It didn't hurt to have friends in low places.

He stopped at the motel long enough to check in, change into a pair of ragged jeans, and kill the spider weaving its web above the window. When he was little, the neighbor kids had tormented him with daddy longlegs and made him cry. Killing spiders was his revenge.

The Purple Onion opened at eight in the morning and didn't close its doors until well after last call at two. It was the kind of place where people with no hope hung out to hide away from reality; where the beer was stale and the whiskey bottom shelf and no one cared. It all drank the same.

Jake took a taxi from the motel to the bar, which he'd scoped out on a previous trip. Driving up to the bar in the bright yellow Charger with racing stripes would mark him as someone to distrust to the regulars. Dented, rusty old cars with cracked glass were the typical vehicles in the parking lot.

It was the average dive bar, long and narrow with old beer ads the only decorations. He got his first whiskey and cola chaser at the bar and took it with him to the beat-up wooden table in the back. The conversations that had dropped when he walked in soon resumed. While pretending to watch the weather on the TV, he studied the other customers.

The tense huddle of three men at the front of the bar didn't match the apathetic atmosphere, but he was too far away to eavesdrop on their conversation. The bartender, a tall skinny man with a small beer gut, had his eye on them even as he chatted with two men at the other end. Jake rotated his glass and wondered what he could grab as a weapon. Standard bar stools didn't work that well in crowded spaces.

But nothing happened, and Jake relaxed enough to get a beer. He didn't want to interfere where he wasn't wanted. The too-perky weather lady predicted a fine, sunny day tomorrow, and he wondered if he should talk

Harmony into playing hooky. They could spend the day playing tourist, as a warmup to nighttime activities.

The time he spent as a bouncer didn't allow him to turn off his instincts, so when the bartender left the bar to speak with an old man at another table, Jake's eyes followed him. The flash of metal reflecting a blinking neon beer sign in the front window had him on his feet and halfway across the room in a second.

"Settle down, Duane," the bartender said, backing up a few feet.

Jake recognized Duane's type. Too skinny, pockmarks in his face, scabs on his arms, shaking so hard Jake didn't know how he remained standing. If Duane was crashing, he became doubly dangerous.

Chairs scraped as other customers moved out of reach of the steak knife Duane waved, aiming at everyone and no one. There'd be no happy ending to the situation, at least as far as Jake foresaw. He circled to get in behind Duane.

"Put down the knife," said one of his friends from several feet away.

"Take it easy," said the other.

Duane didn't pay attention. The weapon traced aimless circles in the air. He advanced two steps closer towards the bartender. "Don," he slurred. "Don cheat me."

"Nobody's cheating anybody," the bartender said. "Put down your knife and go home and sleep it off."

It was easy to predict Duane's next move. Jake had seen it repeated too many times. The druggie lunged at the bartender, but Jake reacted first and grabbed his arm. A dangerous maneuver, because tweakers often found bonus strength out of nowhere. He'd been in fights where it took three bouncers to subdue one meth head. Fate was on his side this time. The knife clattered to the floor, and a kick to the back of his knee ensured Duane did, too.

While all hell broke loose, with everyone yelling at Duane and Duane's friends yelling at everyone else, Jake slipped out the front. He'd established his persona and the bartender was capable of restoring order. If the cops were called, Jake didn't want to be around.

The encounter had left him with an adrenalin high, and he needed to burn off some energy. He considered going to Harmony's place and pounding on her door until she answered. That wouldn't earn him any points, so he started the long, long walk back to the motel.

❋ ❋ ❋

Jake slept in, a rarity. He woke with a clear head but no vision of what came next. He hadn't thought this trip all the way through. His stomach growled and treating Harmony to lunch sounded like a good idea.

He chose a polo shirt and slacks to go with his cover as a successful businessman. The anticipation of seeing the surprise on her face when he showed up had him taking extra care as he shaved.

Once he'd found a parking spot outside the library and verified her car was there, he sent her a text. *Lunch? Mama D's?*

He timed her. At forty-five seconds on the dot, she

rushed out of the front door, stood on the top stair, and looked around. He beeped his horn, climbed out of the Charger, and waved. Even from across the street, he saw her jaw drop. With a swagger in his step, he strode to meet her as she hurried down the stairs.

"Why didn't you tell me you were coming?" Harmony asked as they hugged.

"I wasn't sure I'd make it and didn't want to disappoint you. But the meeting went smoother than I expected, so here I am. Can you take the rest of the day off?"

Her eyebrow lifted. "Play hooky? I haven't done that since high school. I'll have to ask my boss, but I don't see why not. It's slow today. But first, you have to tell me about the car you're driving. What rental company did that come from?"

Jake wished he'd known that a car was the key to her heart. "It's mine. I'll tell you all about it at lunch. Then we can go for a ride, and I'll show you what it's capable of."

Over lunch, at the diner down the street, he spun a tale of finding the Charger in the hills of Georgia. "I didn't expect anything except cobwebs, dust, and snakes, but had to look before we tore down the barn. I claimed the car before any other member of the crew spotted it and without knowing if it could be fixed. It took forever to get the title because the owner was dead."

Harmony wrinkled her nose. "I suppose you drove it out of the barn and took it home."

He groaned. "In my dreams. It took four of us to get it out of the barn and onto the flatbed truck. Then a pal who fixes cars as a hobby spent a year to get it drivable. Finding the parts was a nightmare. We spent the next year doing cosmetic fixes. But it was worth it."

In reality, he'd traded a matching earring and necklace set featuring high-quality sapphires for the pink slip—and fifty dollars, to make it legal. The part about spending time to bring it to its current shape was true, but for reasons other than getting it to run again.

The heavy-duty suspension and brake system masked four hiding spots. A trained dog would sniff them out if they were filled with weed, but Jake refused to deal in drugs. And he'd not met a dog yet who could track down jewelry. He didn't reveal any of that to Harmony.

Jake leaned forward and touched the end of his fingers to the tips of hers. "How was your morning?"

"Today we had story hour. We have a preschool class that comes in every week, and parents bring their little ones in, too. Some weeks I sneak upstairs to watch, but didn't get a chance today. I was working with our high school library aides. A few of them are graduating this year, and I want to make sure they have enough volunteer hours to meet the requirements."

She pulled her hand away and took several bites of her chicken salad sandwich. Jake concentrated on his hamburger.

"We got a new batch of digital books today. I'm looking forward to seeing what's included and if there's anything I haven't read. Ordering them is Janice's job, and she teases me by keeping them a secret."

That was as close as she'd come to talking about

herself. Jake wondered what she was hiding. Not that he could ask. He had his own secrets.

Despite the constant stares, no one bothered them, but too soon the waitress started to clean the nearby tables, a sign she was ready for them to leave. "Still want to go for a drive?" He laid down enough money to cover the bill and a generous tip.

Harmony hesitated. "Would it be okay if I changed clothes first?"

"Do you want me to take you to your place?" he asked as they headed for the door.

"I thought I'd drive George home. You can follow me."

Exactly what he wanted. For more reasons than one. So why did Jake feel no joy? "That works. But drive slow. I don't know my way around. If you go too fast, I might not keep up."

"Like that'll ever happen," she chuckled. "What's your car's name?"

It was his turn to laugh. "I don't even know if the car is a he or a she."

By now they were standing beside it. She put her hands on her hips and circled the Charger. "Maybe it'll tell me later. Anyway, stick with me."


She parked along the curb, and Jake pulled in behind her. Together, they walked to a set of outside stairs that led to the third story. A dog with an obvious German Shepherd heritage snarled at him from inside the fence.

"Meet Piper," Harmony said. "He's got a protective streak a mile wide. It takes a while for him to get used to any newcomers. As long as you're with me, it'll be okay." She reached over the gate and patted the dog and he settled down, but still growled at Jake.

Jake trailed Harmony up the stairs, admiring the view from behind. No wonder she kept a trim figure, climbing these steps every day. He waited patiently as she unlocked the door.

"Let me warn you, it isn't much," she said. "But it's all I need."

*She'd be disgusted if she saw my place.* He nodded. "I'm sure it's fine." He wondered if it was some sort of test. If he reacted badly, would she toss him out?

It wasn't what he'd expected. Was his information wrong? Was there another Harmony Duprie in town? The apartment was small and cluttered by an overabundance of books. The furniture was mismatched and well-used. Still, it was clean and neat in a haphazard way. The front window had an expansive view of the flower garden and the neighbor's yard beyond that. He imagined her cuddling up on the couch and reading to her heart's content.

"Do you want something to drink?" she asked. "I've got pop or iced tea."

He must have passed the test. "Thanks, but I'm good."

"Wait here. I'll be right back." She disappeared down a hallway.

Jake picked up a book from her coffee table—The History of the Northwest American Indians—and flipped through its pages while studying the apartment. There wasn't much to see; a small front room, a tiny kitchen, and the hall that he presumed led to her bedroom. He couldn't reconcile his surroundings with a woman who owned a priceless book. Where did she keep it?

There were three bookshelves in the front room alone. With a random choice, Jake picked the one closest to the window. He started on the top shelf and worked his way down. A few of the titles sounded familiar, but none of them were The Three Musketeers.

"See anything interesting?" she asked, startling him out of his concentration.

"You've got quite a collection here." Jake ran his hand along the spines of the books on one shelf. "Although I've never heard of most of them."

A wide smile lit her face. "I'm a librarian. Books are my passion."

"Have you read all of them?" Jake put the book he held back on the coffee table.

"Not yet. But some I've read two or three times."

He clasped his hands behind his back and studied the second bookshelf. Still no Three Musketeers. "I spend more time reading contracts than make-believe stories." He probably hadn't read a book since dropping out of college.

She stood behind him, and a floral scent wafted over him. He needed to find out what kind of perfume she used and buy her some for her birthday. Whenever that was. Shit. He was so in over his head.

"You know that's a dare," she laughed. "After we go for our ride, I'll pick out a book for you. You have to promise to read at least one chapter, and after that you can decide whether to finish it."

This sounded like fun. "Then I get to challenge you to try something?"

"That's fair. But I get veto power."

So much for his first idea of getting her into bed. He grinned. "I'm open to negotiations. Although I warn you, that's what I do."

He used a quick trip to the bathroom for surveillance. He expected her counter to be cluttered with cosmetics and various beauty products, but there was next to nothing there. Now that he thought about it, she wore little makeup. Another tidbit of information to file away for later use. Without a way to sneak into her bedroom, it was the best he could do.

# Chapter 6

"Do you want to go fast or are you a fan of curvy roads?" Jake tugged on the strap securing Harmony. He was glad he'd cleaned the car before starting the trip and that he'd ditched the fast food wrappers back at the motel.

"Either would be a treat. You've seen what I drive, and as much as I love George, he's only good for slow and steady." Harmony wiggled in the passenger seat of the Charger. "And there are no springs poking through the cushion."

"You need a new car."

"I've had George since I started college. He's a habit I can't shake."

Jake started the Charger and listened to the sweet rumble of the exhaust. "Why do you call your car George?" he asked as he shifted into first and eased down on the gas.

"Remember the cartoon with the Abominable Snowman, and how he always wanted a friend to squeeze and pet and call George? That's how I feel about my car."

Jake stopped himself from laughing. It seemed silly, but she was serious. "Point me to the interstate. I'll show you fast to begin with."

He took it easy at first, not wanting to scare her. But every time he stepped on the gas to zip past another vehicle, her eyes brightened. While watching for flashing blue lights, he pushed the car to go as fast as he could get away with. Not nearly to the top speed it could handle, but enough to impress Harmony.

At an exit forty miles up the road, he pulled off and into a gas station. "Having fun?" he asked, knowing the answer.

"How fast were we going?"

They'd hit one-hundred and ten at one point, but he'd never admit it. "Ninety-five. Do you want a turn?"

Her eyes widened. "You mean it?"

"Absolutely. You drive a stick, right?"

She could. And did. When the speedometer dial reached ninety, he tapped her knee. "Ease up, he said.

"Do I have to?" she asked, sounding like a petulant child, but as the first sign for the Oak Grove exit flashed by, Harmony eased up further on the gas pedal. "I'm not ready to go home yet."

Jake wasn't either, but it was time. "There's a trick to knowing how long you can speed without getting caught, and we're pushing the limit. There's always another day."

The way she'd handled the car, he suspected she'd be a natural at some of the more advanced driving skills he wanted to teach her. A highway patrol vehicle flashed by in the other lanes, giving credence to his statement.

She tapped on the brakes. "How did you know?"

He grinned. "I didn't. Call it instinct."

"How does a guy in the construction business learn these skills?"

He put the back of his hand to his forehead. "It's the remnants of a misspent youth."

She stopped at the bottom of the ramp. "You're a puzzle to me, Mr. Jake Hennessey, and there are too many pieces I can't make fit."

"I guess you'll have to keep me around until you do." But Jake didn't want her to figure him out. It was too dangerous for both of them.

Harmony parked the Charger in front of the house like an expert, a perfect six inches from the curb, but didn't turn off the engine. An awkward silence built a wall between them. She had to make the first move, but waiting made Jake twitchy. The rush of the ride drove his desire for another kind of thrill.

She turned to face him. "Want to come in? I still need to choose a book for you."

He picked up on the tremble in her voice. Did he scare her? Or was it anticipation? "Which one did you have in mind?"

She swung open the car door and got out. "What was the last movie you watched?"

"You won't laugh at me, will you?" He joined her on the sidewalk and deepened his voice. "Bond. James Bond."

"Are you kidding me? I'm a big James Bond fan, too. Sean Connery is my favorite Bond actor. I own the entire series of books, too, although not the first editions. I've read all of them."

Did he remember any of the Bond actors? "I've always thought Pierce Brosnan is underrated. As far as the books go, I don't think I've read any of them."

Harmony reached over the gate to pet the landlords' dog and stop his wild barking. "You make it too easy."

"I only have to read one to beat your challenge and claim my reward," he chuckled.

"I set myself up, didn't I?" She grinned as she unlocked her door.

He waited until they were inside, and the door was closed, to make his move. As she hung her purse on the hook by her door, he snaked his arm around her waist and pulled her against his chest. "That was fun. What do you want to do next?"

She tilted her head up. "What did you have in mind?"

It was the invitation he'd been waiting for. Jake leaned in and gently pressed his lips to hers. His whole body tingled when she deepened the contact. He pulled away before he was satisfied.

"Angel," he groaned, "I don't want to rush things, but kissing you is not enough."

"What are you afraid of?"

He brushed his lips across her forehead. "That I'll fall in love with you and then hurt you. You'll hate me and I'll hate myself if that happens."

"Isn't that the risk we take every time we're attracted

to someone?" Harmony stroked his cheek. "If we don't give it a shot, we'll never know what could be."

He understood taking risks. And getting hurt. What he didn't know was how to love someone. But she was pure temptation.

He took off her glasses, wanting to sink into her deep brown eyes. "You are beautiful."

Her cheeks reddened. "That's sweet of you to say, but I know better."

Jake took a step back and studied her. "Hasn't anyone told you that before?"

"I've heard the words, but I've never believed them." Harmony dropped her gaze towards the floor. "Look at me. I'm a plain Jane. I don't have curves in the right places, my hair is a mousy brown and doesn't flow in the wind, I don't bother with makeup because no one cares at work and when I'm here, it's just me and my books."

Her shoulders stiffened. "Now, can I have my glasses back?"

She reached for them, but Jake held them an arm's length away. "Not until you tell me five good things about yourself," he said.

"Five? That's too many."

Jake remembered the time a friend had challenged him this way. He'd only made it to three, and one had been a lie. "Start with one."

"Easy. I'm smart."

Naive but smart. Jake could live with that. "That's one. And here's a reward." He kissed her on her forehead. "Now, good thing number two."

Harmony raised an eyebrow. "I'm good at my job."

She was taking the easy way out, but it would only go so far. He kissed the tip of her nose. "I'm no expert, but I'll take your word for it. Next."

She clasped her hands together and rested her chin on them. "I don't make a lot of close friends, but the ones I make I stick with forever."

"Loyalty. That's a good one." He ran a finger over her lips, but kissed her chin.

"You're a tease," she nudged his shoulder playfully.

"And I'm waiting for number four."

Harmony hesitated. "I like kids, dogs, and old people?"

"You're pushing it. I'll give you a different one. You have beautiful brown eyes. But you don't get a kiss because I'm the one who said it."

She wrapped her arms around his neck. "Or I need to give you one instead."

He craved the promised kiss but turned his head so it landed on his cheek instead of on his lips. Then he pulled her arms from his neck. Her mouth so close to his was too much of a temptation, and he was playing the long con. "Last one, Angel. Better make it good."

"Why do you call me Angel?"

He grinned. "You're avoiding answering me. Tell me one more good thing about yourself."

With her hands on her hips, she said, "I pay my bills on time and I help my landlords with yard work and cleaning. I donate to several organizations. Are any of those good enough?"

They all were. But he wasn't satisfied. "Is there any

part of your body you're happy with?"

"My hands." She held them out to examine them. "My dad said I had the hands of a pianist. The problem is, I'm tone-deaf."

Reality crashed in. All Jake knew about her parents was that they were dead. He took her hand and caressed the tip of each finger with his lips, trying to recapture the mood. "You have great fingers."

But the moment was lost. Harmony withdrew her hand.

"My mother said they were made for gardening. She was right, because I've kept her African Violet alive." She strode into the kitchen and picked up a pot from the windowsill over the sink. It held a dark green plant with purple flowers which she displayed like a trophy.

"I have a black thumb," he joked. "I'd probably kill it if I touched it."

"That's too bad. I suppose you aren't home enough to take care of one."

"That, and my apartment doesn't have good lighting."

She put the pot back in its place of honor, and Jake struggled to fill the heavy silence. "I'm surprised you don't have more plants."

"Oh, I get my fix helping my landlords with their garden. Did you see how beautiful it is?"

"I missed it while I was busy fending off the vicious dog in the yard."

A smile returned to her face. "There's a trick to making friends with Piper."

He waited. And waited. "Aren't you going to tell me how?"

"Eventually. You'll need to read two books for that."

The crisis had passed, but Jake wasn't sure of what came next. "You haven't even decided on the first one."

"You distracted me."

She'd done the same to him. "You promised me a James Bond."

"True." She grabbed his hand and led him to the bookshelf he hadn't had time to check. "But I didn't say which one."

They sat side by side on the worn-out couch after she'd piled a stack of books on the coffee table.

"I didn't realize there were this many," Jake said, aware of her leg almost touching his. He still hadn't spotted The Three Musketeers, the one book he'd searched for.

She'd shifted into what he labeled her 'teaching' mode. "Ian Fleming wrote the first fourteen, but other authors wrote the rest. I've got all the official ones, and a couple underground take-offs. I think we should start you off with a Fleming story. Did you know that some of the books are based on actual events?"

He reached past her to select a random book, rubbing his arm against hers. His skin tingled at the contact. "How about this one?"

"Nope. Let's start at the beginning. You aren't squeamish, are you? There are a couple of rough scenes." She dug through the stack, intent on finding that one particular book.

Jake doubted they were as rough as some things

he'd lived through. He let a wide smile fill his face. "I'll skip those parts."

"Wimp," she said with laughter in her voice as she placed a worn-out paperback in front of him. "Here you are, Casino Royale. Take care of it. I bought this years ago. And it was used then."

"Does that make it an antique?"

"Nope. Not even a collectible. I'm not that old."

"I'm sorry," he sputtered. "That's not what I meant. I know nothing about old books."

She shook her head, but her lips curled upward. "Keep up. I was teasing you."

How had he missed that? "You didn't mention your sense of humor."

"Most people don't appreciate my sarcasm. I have to be careful to not offend them. So, I don't count it as one of my good points."

"That's too bad. I'll make you a deal. Feel free to express yourself and if I don't understand I won't hold it against you."

She blinked. "We're making a lot of deals, aren't we?"

There was one he hadn't completed. And Jake didn't like to leave a job unfinished. "We made one earlier and I never gave you your reward."

"I thought you changed your mind," she said, shuffling through the stack of books.

He put his hand on top of hers. "Look at me, Angel."

She took so long to react it made him nervous. When she finally did, he couldn't interpret her expression. It was as if she had turned off her emotions.

"I'm an analytical person, Jake. None of whatever

this is between us is logical and it bothers me."

If she had all the details, how he'd tracked her down, she'd understand the logic. But he wouldn't tell her. "It's fate. Coincidence. That's the only explanation."

"Except I don't believe in coincidence."

# Chapter 7

As usual, Harmony's mind was a step ahead of his.

She picked up an armload of the books from her coffee table and carried them to the bookshelf. "There's always a rational explanation for two people getting together. But not us," she said as she returned them to their places. "Why can't I find it?"

Harmony was slipping out of Jake's grasp. Which meant he'd lose his chance at The Three Musketeers, the prize he'd been working for. But the longer he was around her, the more he realized she was the real prize. "Isn't that like asking the meaning of life?" he asked.

"Why are you working in the construction business, Jake?"

The abrupt change in topic sent his mind spinning. "Because I like to eat. Why?"

"You keep going all philosophical on me, and I can't tie the two things together. What would you do if money wasn't an issue?"

He couldn't tell her about the joy he got from a successful heist. "You know what I'd really like to do?

Bring old houses back to life. That's what brought me to Oak Grove. Someone mentioned it during a meeting, and I wanted to check the town out for myself. But the realtor I talked to didn't find any listings I liked. Either that or she didn't understand what I was looking for."

"Sarah? You talked to my friend, Sarah. She's usually on point. I wonder what went wrong. You should talk to her again."

Jake stood and stretched. "Here's a better idea. We can drive around town and sightsee. It'll give me a better idea of what to look for, then we can get some supper."

Harmony's eyes sparkled as she whirled around, abandoning the last book. "Do I get to drive?"

"I've created a monster," he groaned. "Yes, you can drive. On one condition."

"What's that?"

"I get a kiss first."

She put a finger on her cheek and cocked her head. "So, you owe me one as my reward and I owe you one. Do they cancel each other out?"

"Who said your reward was a kiss?"

"True. You never did. But you implied it. It was logical."

He laughed. "Not everything is logical." Jake wrapped his arms around her. "But yes, your reward was going to be a kiss. This way, we both get double the fun."

They moved together—him lowering his head; she raising hers—and their mouths merged in the middle. Her lips tasted as sweet as cotton candy, and Jake's heart beat faster as he pulled her tightly against his chest. Their tongues played tag and no matter how he tried to win control, she matched him move for move until he gave in and let her lead the way.

She broke contact first, pulling away before Jake had a chance to undo her bun. "Does that count as one kiss or two?" she asked, running a finger over his lips.

He grabbed her hand and kissed it as he stared into her eyes. "I lost count. Do we start over?"

"Now we go for that drive and look at houses." Harmony pulled her hand out of his. "You're a temptation I can't allow myself to give into. Not yet."

"You're killing me, Angel. But I'll do it your way."

While she made a trip to the bathroom, Jake paced the small apartment. He'd blown it. There was no way he could steal the book now. He'd gotten too close to his target and doubted she owned the fabled copy of The Three Musketeers, anyway. He'd have to convince himself of it to justify spending so much time with her..

Jake led the way to the car, opened the driver's side door for Harmony, and handed her the keys. "Where are we going?"

"There are a couple of houses to show you. My landlords are considering starting on another property, but haven't committed themselves to a project. We checked out a few houses one weekend, and I thought we could start there."

"I wouldn't want to compete with them," Jake objected while he made sure she fastened her seatbelt.

"They're in the dreaming stage and don't have their hearts set on anything. They have too many things to finish on this house."

Satisfied she was secure, Jake walked around the car and climbed in the passenger's side. It made him uncomfortable, letting her be in control, but he'd promised. She made the right preparations, testing the turn signals and checking the mirrors. Still, he caught himself stepping on a non-existent brake pedal when a car zipped by as she pulled into the street.

"We'll start at the Henderson place. It's from the Victorian era, but has lost much of the style to repairs and remodeling over the years. It would be a great place for someone who wanted it for a family home, but won't attract a flipper. That's probably why Sarah didn't show it to you."

As she drove down the side streets to reach their destination, Jake studied the modest homes with a fresh eye. He always looked for the easy ways to break in and never thought about the people who actually lived in them. But these weren't the homes of people who had money and jewels, and he'd never need to open a window or smash through a basement door of one of them.

By the time they pulled away from the fourth house, Jake decided that his cover story wouldn't work. The funny part was, he'd started to believe it. They drove by several Victorian homes that had been maintained, but none of them were for sale.

"One more," Harmony said as she steered around a sharp curve and started up a hill. "It's the old Aldridge place. People have worked on it before, but they all ran out of money or interest before completing the job. I bet it was gorgeous back in the day."

They turned another corner, and the house popped into view. "It's not on the market," Harmony rambled on, although Jake had stopped listening. "The couple who own it are getting divorced and have to wait for the agreement to be finalized before they can sell the house."

It was coincidence, or Fate playing games with him. Because this was the house he'd spotted on his first trip to Oak Grove. The one that gave him the inspiration for the whole elaborate setup.

The three-story, faded brown-and-tan house desperately needed a paint job and yard work. A window on the second floor was boarded up, and the steps leading to the front porch had no railing. That was the limit of Jake's knowledge about home maintenance. Getting a bank to finance the purchase and money for renovations would be the biggest scam he'd ever pulled.

He'd need to set up a dummy organization. An authentic account with enough cash in it to look legit. That would set him up for his future travels, even if he abandoned the quest for Harmony's book. "Is there a way we can get in?" he asked. Silly question. Of course there was a way. Several that he could spot from the driveway.

"Not until the court closes the case. Then every real estate agent in town will compete to list the house. The husband and wife both live out-of-town now, different towns, and there's no way to reach them to get permission to go inside."

"How do you know that?"

Harmony chuckled. "The Oak Grove gossip mill. Everyone knows everyone's business. They speculate on what they don't know, or make it up. As someone who works with the public, I hear a lot."

That could be hazardous to his long-term plans. "What are they saying about me?"

"I may have dropped a hint about you being a cousin from out of town."

Anyone who saw them kiss would know better. "How long will that work?"

"Not long enough." She shrugged. "It's the downside of living in a small town."

Or he could speed up the timeline. The more people who believed he was in construction, the better. "Is there a restaurant we can go to where people will see us but won't interrupt?"

Harmony scrunched her eyebrows. "Why?"

"Because I want your neighbors to know I'm interested in you. It may be too soon to call us a couple or boyfriend/girlfriend, but I don't want anyone to swoop in and steal you."

"It's not like you have any competition. So many people my age leave for jobs. And you're the best-looking guy I've seen in town for months."

Jake was an expert at giving and receiving compliments. They were part of the game. It was the simple, matter-of-fact way Harmony made the statement that brought heat to his cheeks. He didn't remember the last time he'd blushed. He ran his hand across the top of his head, giving himself a moment to recover his composure. "Why did you stay?"

"It's a long story. I'll tell you over supper."

They ended up at a chain restaurant near the interstate. Enough of the customers were travelers taking a break from their road trip that Jake and Harmony weren't bothered by a constant stream of visitors wanting to say "hi." The food was mediocre but the company he shared it with was top-rate, making the food unimportant.

He let her lead the conversation, realizing she needed time to build up to what he hoped she'd reveal. They discussed the old houses they'd seen, and she told the story of the rise and fall of Oak Grove. Originally a farming community, the steel mills to the south in Pittsburgh and the oil wells to the east had brought in money.

"But there was nothing to support Oak Grove once the mills and the oil industry both died out," she explained. "The town is half the size it used to be. It supported four grocery stores at its peak. Now we're down to one and a half. Even churches have closed."

"Why do you stay?"

She swirled her fork through her spaghetti, but didn't take a bite. "I grew up here. I traveled with my parents as a kid, but always wanted to come back. I chose a college nearby so I could visit on weekends. When my parents died, their friends and my friends helped me get through it. I feel like I owe the town. And then there's the library. Do you know what the Carnegie libraries are?"

"Sorry, no. But I have a feeling I'm about to find out," he grinned.

"Yeah, yeah. Andrew Carnegie was one of the original oil barons and one of the richest men of his time. He did some bad things, but a lot of good things, too. He built libraries all over the place, and the library in Oak Grove is one of them. It's a national treasure, although it's not well known, and I feel honored to work there. People come from all over the country to do research."

She stopped. "I got carried away, didn't I?"

"I asked. Besides, it's clear how much you love your job. Too many people don't. But I didn't see any security guards to protect the books." Was it possible she stored her copy of The Three Musketeers at the library? He'd already mapped two different ways to gain after-hours access.

"We lock the old books room at night, but they aren't worth a lot of money. Their value is in the information they hold. That's why people aren't allowed to check them out, like the book you looked at," she said.

Another theory shot. He tapped his fork against her plate. "Eat before your food gets cold."

While they ate, he prepared himself for her inevitable questions about his own background, trying to spot flaws she might catch. And found none.

"So, where are you from?" she asked.

"Florida, originally. These days I'm based out of Atlanta." Mostly the truth.

"What's Atlanta like? I've never been there."

That made it easy. They spent the rest of the meal discussing various places they'd been. Places they wanted to go.

It was still light when Jake pulled up to the spot

behind Harmony's car. George, he reminded himself. "What do you want to do now?" he asked. "Watch a movie together?"

"My TV broke, and I haven't replaced it." She stared out the windshield. "I have schoolwork to do, anyway."

"I thought you graduated."

"That was my Bachelor's. I'm working on my Masters in a low-residency program."

It sounded impressive. And killed his plan to spend the night. He wasn't sure if he was more eager to get her into bed or have another chance to examine her book collection. "How about tomorrow?"

"Saturday is my housework day. If you want to help me, I'll put you to work."

He wasn't sure what she needed to clean. Her apartment looked spotless. "I leave early on Sunday. Can I see you before then?"

She grimaced. "Do you want to compete with the teenagers at the bowling alley waiting for a lane?"

He raised an eyebrow. "You don't sound enthusiastic."

"I usually spend my afternoon reading."

"That reminds me—I left my book on the coffee table." There was his chance to get her alone. Get another kiss. *And if luck is with me, find The Three Musketeers.*

She must have read his mind. "You stay here. I'll run up and grab it."

He watched her disappear around the corner of the house. What was he doing wrong? She was always a step ahead of him. The naive, small-town librarian had him exactly where he didn't want to be.

# Chapter 8

Jake had one more opportunity to get back in her apartment. When Harmony returned with the book, he met her at the bottom of the outside staircase. The dog was nowhere to be seen, and the house hid them from the road, so there'd be no gossiping eyes to see them.

She paused on the last landing. He imagined the cogs in her brain whirling.

"We never decided on plans for tomorrow," he said casually.

"No, we didn't." She descended the last few stairs as if each were a decision to be made.

"We can go for another ride and spend the afternoon together. Explore the back roads this time. See the countryside." Why was he so desperate to impress her? He had the information he needed to break into her apartment and search for the book.

She stopped on the bottom stair and he had to raise his chin to look her in the face.

"Are you using your car to seduce me, Jake?" she asked.

"If that's what it takes." He hoped she'd take the last step to stand on the concrete with him, but she stayed where she was.

"Interesting strategy. Does it work?"

"I don't know. I've never tried it before."

Harmony touched the tip of her finger to the end of his nose. "Don't you know that your big brown puppy dog eyes are your secret weapon? I'm doing my best to resist them, but it's hard."

He fluttered his eyelashes. "Does this help?"

She moved her finger from his nose to his lips. "Not today. I've set a few rules for my life, and one of them is not having sex this soon. You make me want to break that rule, but it's there for good reasons."

He took the book from her hand. "Then I'll go back to my lonely bed in my lonely motel room and read all by my lonely self. Tomorrow I'll pick you up after lunch and we'll go explore. I might even let you drive. Deal?"

"Another deal?"

Jake grinned. "I have to stop doing that, don't I? Let me try again. Would you like to go for a ride with me tomorrow afternoon? It'll be better than going bowling."

"Anything is better than going bowling," she giggled.

"You're the one who mentioned it. I'm confused."

She lowered her chin, closed her eyes, and put the back of her palm to her forehead. "I was joking. Nobody ever gets my attempts at humor. I give up."

"That's not your fault. You're just smarter than the rest of us." As the words left his mouth, he realized how true they were. What would it be like to have a partner with a brain like hers? But partners were dangerous in his line of work.

"Flattery will get you nowhere," she said.

He knew enough not to argue the point. "At least I tried."

That brought a smile to her face. "See you tomorrow."

"Can I get a goodnight kiss?"

If she'd step off that final stair, they'd be on equal footing, but she stayed where she was, took his face between her hands and gazed into his eyes. When he couldn't take it anymore and was ready to pull her into his arms, she brought her mouth down to meet his. It was a soft kiss, lips only, but it set his senses on fire. Her flowery scent enveloped him, the softness of her hands soothed him, the sweetness of her lips made him hunger for more. He wasn't ready when she pulled away.

"Good night, Jake," she said as she turned and ran up the stairs.

❋ ❋ ❋

*Any other woman I would have followed.* He swirled his bottom-shelf whiskey in the chipped glass, bereft in her absence. Any other woman...

He'd gone back to the hotel after he left her place, even tried to read the James Bond book, but couldn't focus on the story. Somehow, she'd distracted him from asking about the other old books she owned, and he kept repeating the conversation in his head, trying to figure out where he'd gone wrong. So, he'd returned to the

Purple Onion, driving the Charger there but parking a block away.

The bartender recognized him and his first one was free. Jake was on his second and last drink.

The bar seemed busier than the previous night, and Jake assumed it was because of the weekend, but he still snagged a table in the back. There was no Duane in sight, and the atmosphere felt friendlier. Jake wasn't there to make friends but instinct kept him alert to everything going on. It was the learned skill of his time working as a bouncer. Which was why he was aware of an undercurrent of tension. And the bartender keeping an eye on him.

It was up to the bartender to make the first move.

Jake finished his drink and set down his glass. He debated going to the bar and getting a third. He wasn't ready to face the empty motel room, but less ready to fend off curious cops.

"You want another?" asked the bartender as he cleaned the trash off a nearby table.

"I would, but the police monitoring the place wouldn't be happy about me driving later." Jake shrugged. "Unless they got bored and are gone."

"Some of the guys have you pegged as a cop after last night."

"No, just an out of work bouncer."

"You're not from around here."

"Nope. From Atlanta. The bar got bought out and the new owners are turning it into a martini club." Jake grimaced. "Martinis. I don't fit into their image."

"Not much work for a bouncer here."

"I figured that out. I thought I had a job lined up in Pittsburgh, but it fell through. Chicago is my next possibility, but I have time to kill between here and there. This seemed like one of those scenic little towns my mother always talks about, so I stopped to take pictures for her. I'll be heading out tomorrow."

"If you run into Mitch Waterberg up there, tell him Cranberry says hey."

"Will do." Jake stood, took a couple of bills out of his wallet, and tossed them on the table. "Thanks for the drink. If I'm ever back in town, I know where to come."

Outside, Jake stopped to check if the cops were still parked nearby. They were, which gave Jake confidence no one had messed with the Charger. Normally, he would have checked that there wasn't someone waiting to ambush him, but he hadn't made any enemies locally.

The car was around the corner, but that didn't mean the cops would let him off the hook. After starting the engine, and with the lights turned off, he waited. Sure enough, it didn't take long for the unmarked vehicle to cruise down the street. Once it was out of sight, Jake turned on his headlights and headed back to the motel.

Overall, it had been a successful night. He'd established his reputation and made a contact. It was always a good idea to have friends in unlikely places. It had saved his butt a time or two.

Once he was in his room, he turned on the TV,

flipped to an old movie for background noise, and picked up the James Bond book.

❊ ❊ ❊

Jake slept in late but showed up just after noon to Harmony's apartment. He hoped to have solo time with her book collection. Although he had the suspicion she didn't take as long to get ready as most women, he'd have to work with what she gave him.

Luck was with him, because she was dressed in her oldest jeans, the ones with numerous rips, and wanted to shower and change clothes. He jokingly offered to help her but didn't take offense when she turned him down. He sat down with his book and the cup of coffee she gave him and told her to take as long as she needed.

When he heard the water running, he began his methodical search. Shelf by shelf, he read the title of each book, even the ones he'd already looked through. He could rearrange the books to fill in the space left by the one he stole, and it would be weeks or months before she noticed its absence.

Halfway through the second bookshelf, it registered that the water was no longer running. He was out of time.

Any other woman would have applied her makeup next, giving him the chance to look through the third bookshelf. Not Harmony. He settled back into his spot on the couch, picked up his book, and flipped to the page where he'd left off.

When she emerged from her bedroom, Harmony

was coiling her hair into its bun, and Jake wondered how long it was. He wanted to stop her and ask her to let it hang freely.

"Where should we go?" he asked as he followed her down the stairs.

"There's some beautiful farmland north of town. Green pastures, old-fashioned farmhouses. Barns with chewing tobacco ads still painted on the sides. How does that sound?"

"Scenic. Like a tourism board commercial. How are the roads?"

"Paved, mostly. Hilly and curvy. Is that all right?"

He nodded. "Sounds like fun and the perfect opportunity to test the Charger's suspension. You can act as my navigator until I can check out what we're getting ourselves into."

"I'll get a turn?" she asked as they reached the bottom.

"Absolutely. I might even show you a trick or two." She could be his getaway driver, not that he'd ever needed one. No, he wouldn't involve her in his business. It was too risky for the both of them.


He mapped the roads in his head as she directed him where to go. It was an ability he hadn't known he had or wanted until the first time he ran from the cops as a teenager and had gotten away by using a narrow path between two buildings. Now, it was like every twist and turn embedded itself in his brain. A friend compared it to those rare people who read a book and remember every word, only he created a map of potential hiding places and escape routes.

They came across a spot that was laid out with straight roads, like a city streetscape with no houses.

"What's this?" he asked, pulling to the side.

Harmony quirked her mouth. "We call it Hannigan's Folly. Seven or eight years ago, a developer bought some land, got the permits, put in the roads, and ran out of money. Never put in the utilities. We don't know who would have bought this far from town, anyway. It's not close enough to the interstate for commuters, and the lots aren't big enough for hobby farmers. So, it sits here, crumbling, except for this street that the county maintains because it joins two other roads."

"And no one ever comes here?"

"Except for parents teaching their kids to drive and the occasional drug dealer, no."

Exactly what he was looking for.

They spent the next hour practicing driving skills. Harmony had the basics, but her technique needed refining to match the abilities of the Charger. A too-sharp twist of the steering wheel could end in a ditch on the side of the road. A missed shift might not hurt in her old car, but it could be a disaster in a getaway chase.

He never used his car on jobs, anyway. The bright yellow was too distinctive. He rented cars under fake names as much as possible. The managers of small privately-owned lots were often willing to take money under the table. The major car rental companies were his last resort.

The last shift she made turned out sloppy. Not

bad enough to grind the gears, but the car lost speed. "Getting tired?" Jake asked.

"I haven't driven this much in a long time. Pittsburgh is about as far as I go, and I won't take George there anymore. He's not up to it," Harmony admitted. "But while this has been fun, I feel like your car can do more."

"It can. But you aren't ready for the advanced tricks."

"Like what? Can you show me?"

"Not today," he said. "We have company."

A maroon minivan had parked on one of the cross streets. An older man and a teenage boy climbed out and changed places, so the boy sat in the driver's seat.

"If we stay, we'll make the kid nervous. The last thing I wanted when I learned to drive was an audience." Harmony reached to unfasten her seatbelt.

Jake put out his hand to stop her. "Are you in a hurry to return?"

"No."

"Is there a back road that will avoid town and bring us in on the other side? Does such a road exist?"

She stroked the steering wheel. "Are you okay with dirt part of the way?"

He'd have to stop and wash his car before leaving tomorrow, but that was a minor inconvenience. "Sounds like an adventure. Do you want to drive or are you ready for me to take over?"

They swapped places, with Jake driving and Harmony playing navigator. The route was long with a million curves, few crossroads, and fewer hiding spots, which made it unfit as an escape path. But the scenery was interesting and the company enjoyable, so Jake ranked the drive in the plus column. As he steered the Charger around yet another curve and over a pothole, he guided the conversation back to Harmony's books. With one particular book in mind.

"I'm curious," he said in a moment of quiet as they drove past yet another scenic farm, "What do you do when you run out of room for new books?"

"Buy a new bookshelf." She had a grin on her face that stretched from ear to ear. "I put one in the bedroom a few months ago."

He still hadn't seen that room. "Is that where you keep your most valuable books?"

"No, those are my comfort books. Old favorites I can grab and reread a few pages if I wake up in the middle of the night."

He was getting nowhere in the hunt for his prize.

"But I have been known to give books away on rare occasions," she continued.

He cocked his head. "That was sarcasm, right?"

"Wow. I'm impressed. You catch on quickly. Turn left here. It's the dirt road I warned you about."

For dirt, it was in decent shape. No major dips or ruts, but Jake slowed down so he wouldn't create a dust storm. "What do you really do with your old books?"

"There's a nursing home I donate them to. If I end up with duplicates—don't laugh, it happens—I give them to the hospital."

"How do you end up with two of the same?" Jake was truly curious.

"Companies will change the book's cover and I

think it's a different book. Sometimes, they change the title, and I don't realize it's the same story. It happens when the author makes revisions and re-releases it. They'll put a warning about the new name in small print somewhere and hope no one sees it."

"That doesn't sound fair."

She shrugged. "Then you have the authors that release an erotic and sweet version of the same story. Makes things confusing."

"I don't even know what that means," Jake chuckled.

"Sorry." She stared straight ahead. "Sweet means no sex scenes, not even any heavy foreplay." Her cheeks turned bright red. "We don't qualify."

He loved pushing her out of her comfort zone. "And the other one?"

The red deepened on her face. "Erotica? We don't qualify for that, either, since we haven't had sex yet."

"That's easy to fix," he suggested. His pulse sped up.

"You're leaving tomorrow."

"We have all night."

"I don't do one-night stands, Jake. And I don't know if you'll ever come back."

# Chapter 9

Jake didn't know if he'd make it back to Oak Grove. Not when he'd been unable to locate the book, and with a Sarasota cop five feet away from a house he'd broken into.

Getting in had been easy. The owners had an overly-friendly dog and they'd left the doggy-door in the back entrance unfastened. Their weekly housekeeper, a heavy-set older woman who he'd spent several hours plying with alcohol and attention, had given him the basic details of the layout. He'd lured the cocker spaniel outside with bacon-flavored treats, then picked the lock on the back door.

The housekeeper hadn't mentioned the motion-detection system in the living room. It hadn't triggered when he went upstairs to the second floor but sounded as he came back down with the topaz and gold jewelry in a small bag tucked inside his shirt. He must have brushed through a stray beam.

Jake had covered his tracks by locking the back door on the way out. An expert could spot the scratch marks left behind by his tools, but first, they needed to look for them.

He made it outside before the cops arrived, and almost to the neighbor's yard. Now, covered by the darkness of night, he crouched behind a bush, hoping the spaniel didn't want his attention. Luckily, the pooch was busy trying to get the cop to play fetch with a rubber squeaky toy.

The cop's radio squawked. He held a quick conversation, then was joined by a second officer. With the dog at their heels, they rattled the knob on the back door. It held firm. But the dog dashed inside through the doggy door and emerged with a different toy in its jaws.

The officers shone their lights inside through the window. "It all looks good," the first officer said. "Do you suppose the dog set off the system?"

"We'll have to wait until the owners get here to find out." The second cop reached down to pet the dog. "But it looks like a false alarm. Wouldn't be the first time it happened."

Jake wasn't in the clear. Soon, the pooch might get bored and look for a new playmate, revealing his hiding spot. Luckily, he hadn't drugged the animal, because that would have alerted the officers to something being wrong.

The June night was unseasonably warm, and beads of sweat rolled off Jake's forehead and dripped into his eyes. He didn't dare move to wipe them off. He'd always hated Florida weather. Worse, Florida mosquitoes. One buzzed near his ear and he couldn't swat it. He had to wait while the cops conferred in low voices he couldn't hear, the second one petting the dog the entire time.

They moved around the corner of the house, with the dog following them, wagging its tail. Like a jack in the box springing free, Jake darted from behind the hibiscus and leaped over the fence to the neighbor's yard. From there, he dashed to the alley and down to where it joined the main street. He paused long enough to pull off his mottled black shirt to reveal a blue t-shirt and catch his breath. Down the street, a dog barked. A symphony of other dogs joined in.

The rental car wasn't far away. If he got to it before more police showed up, he'd be safe. He rotated his shoulders to ease the tension and headed towards it at a normal walking pace. Just a man out for an evening stroll.

The wail of sirens got closer as he reached the car. He unlocked it, and climbed in, but didn't start the engine. First, he wiped off the sweat, scratched a mosquito bite, then called the motel. Somehow, he'd gotten lost and needed directions. If the cops questioned him, he'd have an alibi.

But no police vehicle came down the street. After delaying for fifteen minutes, he started the trip back to his room, where a bottle of whiskey waited. It would soothe the adrenalin surging in his veins.


Even the booze didn't help him sleep. He turned on the TV and picked up the James Bond book he'd bought on a whim. He'd returned Harmony's, because he'd been afraid he'd lose it somewhere, but when he spotted this copy at a convenience store, he didn't resist. That way, if he ever saw her again, he could say he'd finished it.

He'd sent her a couple of postcards of places where he'd been, and one small bouquet of pink tulips. So far, he'd avoided calling her. She deserved someone better than him, although she wouldn't find that guy in Oak Grove.

The proceeds from the jewels would help fund buying the house if it ever hit the market. The stones were valuable on their own, but they also had ties to the early Spanish inhabitants of the Saint Augustine area, and the historical value was the real prize. A collector had made it known that he was willing to pay a premium price for the pieces, and Jake aimed to please.

❋ ❋ ❋

The customers of Atlanta's Shaggy's Bar were well-behaved for a Friday night. Marty and Jake were keeping an eye on the bunch outside, smoking. They'd heard the rumor about one guy selling ecstasy and needed to shut him down. Jake would be happy if the gossip turned out to be false.

"You smell that, man?" Marty shifted his feet, lifted his nose in the air and sniffed. He didn't look like a fighter, all awkward angles, but his reputation for crowd control was unmatched. Jake was glad to back him up as the bar's bouncer anytime.

"Like someone is hanging over your shoulder? Keep it clean tonight, buddy. No bribes—er, tips—no asking the pretty girls for kisses. The only thing I can figure out is that the boss is watching."

"What did you do on your days off? I keep nagging the boss to put you on full time, but can't talk him into it." Marty reached down and snagged an empty cigarette pack off the ground and tossed it in the nearby trash can.

*Besides stealing a necklace?* "I registered my company with the Georgia Secretary of State." Sometimes the truth was stranger than fiction. The process had been easier and cheaper than Jake had expected. He regretted having to use an actual credit card, but he couldn't avoid it. The next step was to get business cards.

Marty chuckled. "Good one. What does your business do?"

"Flips old houses. I hear it's the thing to do these days."

"What do you know about construction?"

"I've been watching that TV show. It doesn't look hard." Jake jerked his chin towards the smokers. He'd spotted a handshake covering an exchange of cash and a little baggy. "And action."

Marty plowed through the gathering and stopped inches from the offending men. "That's your third offense, Rock. You're banned. Get off the premises."

"It was just some vitamin C, Marty, my man," the dealer, a heavy-set guy, said. "No need to get your panties in a bunch."

Marty folded his arms and stared at the dealer. Jake stood a few feet behind him, ready to spring into action.

"Five," Marty said. "Four."

Jake inched closer.

"Three."

The dealer gave it one last try. "Dude, it was nothing."

"Two."

Jake took another step.

"One."

The dealer hesitated. Marty reached out and poked him in the chest. "Time's up."

Looking around for support and finding none from the group, the man backed up and raised his hands to shoulder-height. Good thing, because the tightness in Marty's back showed through his shirt. He'd been ready to take the guy down hard.

"I'm leaving," the dealer muttered, as he turned and jogged down the sidewalk.

Jake tapped the customer on his shoulder. He wasn't a regular, so Jake wouldn't give him any slack. "You, too."

The overweight man opened and closed his mouth but decided whatever he was going to say wasn't worth it. He pushed his way past Jake and headed the opposite way from the dealer. "This place sucks."

Marty didn't wait until he was gone to ask, "Anyone want to join 'em?"

The rest of the smokers didn't move, except to take puffs off their cigarettes. "I was hoping you'd get to kick his ass," one of them said. "It would have taken all of a single punch from either of you guys."

Jake needed to make a score to ease the adrenalin surging in his veins. Not drugs, but jewelry, even a slim silver necklace. He moved back to the podium by the door while Marty chatted with the group. The tingle at the base of his neck hadn't gone away. The last time he'd felt like this, the bar he was at had been under surveillance by undercover cops. There were none to be seen tonight, which meant if they were there, they were good at their jobs. No jewelry would go missing this night, at least not any ending up in his pocket.

A young couple arrived and Jake triple-checked their IDs. The girl's long brown ponytail made him wonder how long Harmony's hair really was, once she uncoiled it from its bun. He still had hopes he'd find out one of these days.

He thought about calling her. But it was late, and she was probably asleep. Or out on a date. That would be her best choice.

❋ ❋ ❋

Another night, another dive bar. But Jake was a customer, on the hunt for his old friend Ben. He'd caught a news report about smash and grab thefts happening at local pawnshops. He didn't know if it was the copycat or Ben, and tracking Ben down in the type of bars he preferred was a game of chance. Especially in a town as big as Atlanta.

Curiosity drove him, as much as wanting to warn Ben about a possible competitor. That's what Jake told himself. Deep down, he recognized he wanted to have a drink and swap stories with someone who knew his background. Someone he didn't have to pretend for.

The old man who taught him the fine art of jewelry theft had been that for a few years. He was a skinny guy who went by the name of Grimm. In the early years, Grimm would check in on Jake every few months, then he got caught in a sting operation, trying to steal a jewelry shipment from a warehouse. Last Jake heard, Grimm was in a nursing home. Prison had broken him.

Jake finished his first drink in Grimm's honor. Ben wasn't in this bar, but it was early. He'd have a couple of drinks and see what happened.

The trio of men wearing hoodies at the bar made him twitchy. His bouncer instincts insisted they were up to something, and he couldn't figure out what. But the bartender, a large black man, was the king of his establishment and he didn't seem bothered, so Jake sat in his dark corner, drank his stale beer, and waited. He'd scoped out the back door, so if things turned ugly, he had a way out.

By eleven, he was bored. By eleven-thirty, he was ready to leave, go home, and get some sleep. At midnight, he stood, prepared to head outside and call a taxi.

The trio at the bar had different plans for him. Without turning around, Jake sensed he was being followed. The other customers refused to meet his eyes, confirming his suspicion. Two he could handle. Three was pushing it, especially if they had weapons. If they had guns, he was a dead man.

He stopped inside the front door, pretending to read a flyer posted on the window. In the dim reflection, a flash of light confirmed Jake's fear. At least one of them had a knife. He turned to face them.

"Y'all have a problem?" he asked in the broadest Southern accent he could fake.

The direct confrontation confused them. Jake guessed they preferred to catch their victims in the dark alleys, where they'd work unseen. It wasn't the first time he'd dealt with that mentality, and Jake had the scars to prove it.

The tension in the bar was as thick as the rain in the middle of a hurricane. Jake waited for one of the punks to make the first move. The only motion was the shortest and skinniest of the three tapping his fingers against his thigh, itching to reach for his blade. Jake watched the punk's eyes.

Their narrowing signaled the attack. Jake reacted lightning-fast, twisting to avoid the shiv. A heartbeat later, his fist thudded into the short man's face. The weapon clattered to the floor, but Jake had no opportunity to retrieve it. A shoulder rammed into his chest, sending him staggering backwards.

He smashed against the door, caught himself, and plunged forward, aiming low. Street fighting didn't have rules. Or morals. His next blow met the soft belly of an attacker. He followed it with the heel of his hand shoved into the solar plexus. His attacker fell to his knees, gasping for breath. One down. For now.

Not good enough. Working on instinct alone, Jake threw his body to the right, shoulder first, and rammed into a solid mass of muscle. A sting in his forearm didn't stop him from thrusting an elbow into his opponent's side. A fist brushed against his jaw, but it barely jarred his head. He answered with an uppercut. The punk slumped against the bar.

One to go. An arm wrapped around his neck, cutting off his air. The first guy, back on his feet, jammed a fist in Jake's face, and drew back for a second swing.

Jake reached behind himself and grabbed his captor by the ears. Then he pushed off and threw himself forward. His head bored into the first punk's stomach, dragging along the guy from behind, but a rush of warmth from his side indicated a second knife had found its target. The trio ended up in a tangled knot on the floor. Jake extricated himself first, with the assistance of random punches and kicks, staggered to his feet, and tried to catch his breath.

"You don't stand a chance against the three of them," said a voice to his right. Jake recognized it as the bartender's.

"Nope. But I figured I'd make the shitheads work for it."

"I think they've had enough fun for the night." He thunked a baseball bat against the bar, then pointed it at the trio. "I want you three out. And the next time I see your faces in here, you better be carrying bibles and singing hymns. Now, out." He pointed the bat towards the door.

Bibles and hymns? Jake liked the bartender's sense of humor. He would have grinned as the punks limped out the door, but his mouth hurt. At least one blow had met its mark.

"You want another drink?" the bartender asked.

"Yeah, that and a spare towel or two, if you have any. I don't want to drip all over your floor."

A gray cloth tumbled through the air. Jake caught it and held it to his side. "You need to see a doc?" the bartender asked.

"Naw, it isn't deep. Just a new scar to add to my collection. I'll throw some bandages on it when I get home."

"Your call."

"Was that a gang initiation or something?"

The bartender shrugged. "Dunno. I've never seen those assholes before. But they're too old to be joining a gang. More likely they figured you were a soft touch."

*True. Or whoever was watching him sent the men to scare me off. But from what?* He needed to get home and stand under a hot shower for as long as he could. Hopefully, the landlord hadn't turned off the water heater again.

# Chapter 10

Ten minutes ago, Harmony's elderly landlords had pulled out of the driveway in their pickup, the dog bouncing around in the front seat. Jake had spotted Harmony leaving earlier, off to her Wednesday night get-together with her friends. It provided the perfect opportunity to scope out the bookshelf in her bedroom. Yet, he sat here, parked across the street in a beat-up rental, wasting time.

He'd driven by the old house first. Still no for sale sign. But if he grabbed the book and got out of town, he wouldn't need the excuse of remodeling it. That way, he'd never see her face when she discovered the book missing, or hold her to comfort her. Fool. The smart move was to walk away.

The lock on her door was an upper-end model, a newer brand he'd never picked. It should be a simple job, but he wouldn't find out until he tried.

He drove to the convenience store a few blocks away and parked, headed inside, and bought a scratch-off ticket. Lost, of course, but that wasn't a shock. Then he took a walk, ending up in the alley behind her place.

Anticipation burned in his veins as he ran up the steps. She'd forgotten to leave her outside light on, but he worked by touch and sound. The pick slid into the mechanism and he twisted it, learning the inner workings. It wasn't the hardest lock he'd ever worked on, but enough of a challenge to satisfy his cravings. The soft click when the pins fell into place felt like winning a gold medal.

He opened the door, listening to make sure the apartment was empty and his to ravage. Then he engaged the lock, stepped outside, and closed it behind him. A practice run. He didn't know how long the landlords planned to be gone, and he needed time to explore.

That's the excuse he told himself, in his shabby motel room in Pittsburgh. He thought about showing up in the morning and inviting her to breakfast. But he'd have no explanation for the bruise that marred his face or the swath of bandages on his arm. His shirt covered the wound on his side. He'd send her flowers instead, unless he talked himself out of it. In the meantime, an amethyst necklace in Cincinnati called his name.

❊ ❊ ❊

"You run into a wall?" Marty chuckled, studying Jake's face.

Jake grimaced. "Three of them. Call it two and a half. One went down too easy."

It was a slow night, with a hint of a cooling breeze, but the shadow lurking across the street had Jake on edge.

"How many do you see?" Marty asked after checking the IDs of a group of college kids. He jerked his chin in the shadow's direction.

"Only the one. But he's been there for forty-five minutes."

"The not-so-friendly neighborhood drug dealer back?"

"I haven't seen him talk to anyone." Jake shrugged. "He's walked around the corner a few times, and I've lost track of him. And this person is a lot smaller." The hoodie the shadow wore bothered Jake. One of the gang out for revenge?

"He's not trying to hide, either." Marty pointed out. "That's what bothers me. Almost like he's daring us to go talk to him."

"Or setting us up for an ambush."

"You got an enemy?"

*Bunches of them, on both sides of the legal fence.* Jake chuckled. "If I made it this far in life without an enemy or two, I wouldn't really be living, right?"

"That's one way of looking at it. If you're good, I'm going to make the rounds inside. It's plenty quiet, but gotta keep the boss happy by showing my face."

Most nights, checking IDs kept the bouncers busy. Marty's reputation chased the worst of the riffraff away. "Say hi to that pretty girl you flirted with earlier," Jake grinned.

"Her?" Marty snorted. "Dude, you've lost your touch. The only guy she checked out was you. I'll tell her you say hey."

All Jake remembered about her was her bleached

blond hair and heavy makeup. Not his type anymore. He had his sights set on a brunette. "You do that," he said. "Maybe I'll get lucky." It was all part of the game.

With nothing better to do, Jake grabbed a broom to sweep up the cigarette butts that littered the sidewalk. At the same time, he kept his eyes on the figure across the street.

He stopped to check the IDs of two new arrivals. When he checked again, the shadow had disappeared. That didn't settle his nerves. He wondered if Marty had a stalker, or a secret admirer.

The idea amused him. He hadn't practiced his limited trailing skills for months. He'd gather what information he could before sharing it with Marty. Starting tonight, if the shadow returned.

Jake had explored the side streets and alleys near the bar, but the shadow took him further than normal.

Like a bee drawn to spring flowers, the stalker had returned a few minutes after Marty came back outside. Jake had assumed the shadow lived in an apartment across the street, but they were now five blocks away and the unfamiliar territory made him unhappy. Still, as he slipped from behind one car to the next, he didn't think he'd been spotted.

He'd left early, not telling Marty of his plan. From his hiding spot a block away, he'd waited until the bar closed and Marty headed inside. The routine never changed. Marty would chat with the bartender until the money was counted and locked in the safe. Then he'd exit out the back door, where he parked.

The stalker didn't wait that long. He started the trek as soon as the front door closed for the night. Jake didn't understand what he was up to.

Six blocks from the bar, the figure headed down a narrow break between two dilapidated apartment buildings. If Jake followed, and the stalker turned at the wrong moment, there'd be no hiding. But he'd come this far and wouldn't give up.

By the time Jake crossed the street, he'd lost sight of his prey. He peered down the path, barely wide enough for him to fit through, but didn't see anything in the dark tunnel. A small light attempted to brighten the other end, so it wasn't a trap—he hoped. He slid along one wall, pretending he belonged.

A tiny courtyard graced the end of the tunnel, with a single overhead light in the middle. But the lights from the surrounding apartments cast streams of dim illumination and spread an eerie glow. In one of those rays, Jake saw a figure struggling with a window in the basement level. It had to be his quarry.

Jake decided to forgo quietness for speed as he dashed across the courtyard before the shadow entered the building. He grabbed the figure by the shoulder as he knelt to slide, head-first, into the basement.

"What are you up to?" Jake asked.

Light reflected in wide eyes. "Be quiet, you'll wake Mom."

What? That wasn't the reaction Jake expected. He nodded, put his fingers to his lips, and pointed his chin to a bench a few feet away.

They sat in silence for a few minutes while Jake studied the person, unsure if they were male or female. Boy or girl was more like it, because he suspected he or she was a young teen. Tall for the age, too thin, but the face showed no sign of whiskers. Jake waited for them to break the silence and spill their guts.

"I suppose you wonder what I was doing," they said. The voice didn't hold any clues to the identity of the teen.

Jake nodded.

"There's a story to that. Mom said the other guy is my dad, and I'm trying to work up the courage to talk to him. She doesn't want me to, so I have to sneak out after she's asleep." The kid's mouth formed a tight line. "And when I say asleep, I mean so drunk she can't stay awake."

Shit. Jake had been that kid. He held out his hand. "I'm Jake. You are?"

The kid shook it. "I'm Alex."

No help there in identifying which sex the kid was. They could be Alexander or Alexandria. "Marty never mentioned having a kid."

"He doesn't know. Mom never told him."

That complicated things.

"What are you going to say to Marty when you talk to him?"

"Dunno. I mean, it's not like he's a fairy godmother or anything. He works in a bar. How much money can he have? That's what I used to think when I was younger. When I found my dad, he'd swoop in and rescue me, and we'd live happily ever after. Kid stuff, ya' know. Now..."

Alex shrugged. "It would be nice if he knew I existed. We could talk some days. Grab a burger together or something."

"How would you feel if he doesn't want to talk to you?"

The kid kicked at the stubble of weed by their foot. "That's the problem."

One Jake didn't have any idea how to solve. Marty had never mentioned wanting a family.

"How d'ya find me?" Alex asked.

"If you were trying to hide, you weren't doing a very good job. It was easy to follow you."

"Not like that other guy, huh? I try, but he's great. I've picked up a few things from watching him."

Every muscle in Jake's body tightened. He took a deep breath and forced himself to relax. "What guy is that?"

"I think he's a cop. At first, it seemed like he was making sure you guys weren't dealing drugs or something. Then I figured out he only stuck around on nights you were there. You owe somebody a bunch of money?"

"Not me."

"Huh."

"What does the dude look like?"

"About your height. Not skinny, but he doesn't have your muscles. Always wears black. He sits in a car down the street from the bar. Gets out every now and then to stretch."

The description didn't narrow the list of suspects down any. Could be the feds, a private investigator, or he'd stepped on a competitor's toes without knowing it.

None of which he could share with Alex. "Sounds like I have a secret admirer."

The giggle he got in response convinced Jake that Alex was a girl, adding another issue. Marty might be able to handle a teenage boy, but a girl?

"Make you a deal. I'll keep an eye on him and you get my dad to talk to me."

Not a trade Jake wanted to make. "Stay away from the guy in black. He sounds like bad news. I'll break the ice with Marty. You realize he might not be your dad, don't you?"

"You mean my mom lied to me?" She shrugged. "Story of my life. But he looks like me, dontcha think?" She turned towards Jake.

Trick question. "It's too dark to tell." He studied her face, but it didn't tell him much. The goth makeup she wore made her look older than she sounded. But maybe that's what she was shooting for.

"Can you talk to him tomorrow?" Alex asked.

"Saturdays are busy, so I won't make any promises."

She grimaced. "I've waited so long. All my life."

Jake hid his grin. Typical young teenager. It made him happy she still had the childlike ability to hold onto hope. Life had beaten that phase out of him too fast.

# Chapter 11

The motel was several steps above the normal places Jake stayed. If he talked Harmony into going to bed with him, he wanted a decent place to take her. He'd come to the unsupported conclusion that she was afraid of the reaction if her landlords overheard their activities.

Before leaving Atlanta, he'd called to tell her he was coming and to see if she could take time off. He had four days free and hoped to spend as much of the time with her as possible, courtesy of finally receiving payment for that emerald ring. When he returned home, he'd meet with Alex and figure out the next step to connect her with Marty.

Harmony had texted him a few days earlier to tell him the old house was on the market, giving him the excuse he needed for this trip. He had his business cards and bank account, thanks to a well-paid acquaintance with access to banking records. Everything was in place.

He'd taken his car to a different contact for maintenance. The oil needed to be changed, and the undercarriage checked for trackers. They'd found nothing suspicious, but he still assumed the man in black that Alex mentioned was from the FBI or another law enforcement agency.

Establishing himself as a legit business owner would provide additional coverage for his main alibi. In the last few weeks, he'd become addicted to those home repair shows and even gone to a big box store for a class in basic building repairs. He'd learned a few things, including how to get into a window with its frame painted shut.

He made it into town late because of road construction in West Virginia. Tonight, he'd hit up the Purple Onion and let her sleep. If he worked his magic correctly, she wouldn't get any rest for the next two nights.

His favorite bartender was on duty, and Jake nodded to him while surveying the small assortment of customers. No Duane in sight, and the knot of tension in Jake's back released. By the time he got to the bar, a whiskey waited for him.

"Didn't get that job in Chicago?" the bartender asked as Jake paid for his drink.

"Nope. A friend of a friend got me a spot with another bar in Atlanta. At least I saw new parts of the country on the trip, so it wasn't a total waste."

"So, what brings you back here…?"

He knew the dance. "Jake," he said. No handshake was expected. "My mom asked me to get her some more pictures. She got it in her head this would be a good place to retire."

"Carl," the bartender offered. "And unless your mother likes snow and lots of it, she might want to think again."

"Thanks for the advice. I'll tell her." Jake nodded and strolled to the little table in the back corner to watch customers come and go. That was enough for the night. It was still too soon for him to be trusted. And anything illegal wasn't likely to happen out here in the public area. He suspected the real action happened in a private office behind a locked door.

※ ※ ※

Jake shifted the flimsy cardboard box containing pastries from Oak Grove's bakery under his arm. He'd timed his arrival with her normal schedule, even if she had the day off to spend with him. Softening her up with goodies was a good way to start it.

He didn't expect to find Harmony in her robe, sitting on her steps, patting the dog, drinking coffee, and reading the local paper. She'd already pulled her hair into its characteristic bun, and he felt a twinge of disappointment that he'd missed seeing it undone. He cleared his throat and she looked up, almost spilling her drink.

"Jake! I didn't think you'd be here this early."

"I come bearing gifts." He held out the box. "I'm told these are the best in town."

"Stublers? Tell me you got your hands on an apple fritter."

Jake pulled the box back before she could take it. "Sorry, no, but I got these cinnamon rolls. Do I need to return them?"

Her mouth formed an 'O.' "Who did you bribe to

get those? Do you know how fast they sell out?"

He'd remember that for another day. "I only got three. That's all they had. One for you, one for me, and one to share. Will that work?"

"We'll want fresh coffee to go with them." She stood, and, remembering her outfit, pulled her robe closed.

He wondered what more it would take to get it off her.

"I'll be right back. You stay here and keep Piper company."

The dog growled softly, but Jake put down the rolls and reached into his pocket. He'd brought along some doggy goodies, too. Bacon-flavored ones. He tossed one to Piper, hoping the pooch would find it irresistible.

It worked. By the time Harmony returned, fully dressed, Jake was sitting on the steps, reading the newspaper with Piper resting his head on Jake's thigh, waiting to be patted. "I'd come help you," he said, "but my new friend doesn't want to move."

"You've passed the test," she joked. "But it's time for him to go back in the yard so we can enjoy the rolls without him slobbering all over them."

She set down the cups, swooped up the dog, and dropped him over the fence before Jake had a chance to move. The lady was stronger than she looked. Piper ran off to roll in a patch of grass.

After picking up her coffee cup and handing Jake his, she settled on the stair beside him. "Ready for a bit of heaven?" she asked, while reaching for the bakery box.

The clear blue skies, the scent of fresh coffee, the pretty girl sitting next to him. It was so sitcom-perfect that Jake wondered where the TV cameras were hidden. "Sure. But I don't expect they'll taste as good as you look." He'd decided to try a constant string of compliments to soften her up. Had any of her previous boyfriends ever treated her the way she deserved?

A reddening of her cheeks was his reward. That, and the cinnamon roll she plated and handed to him. "I can warm it in the microwave if you want," she said.

Based on the amount of sticky goop that dripped over the top, heating up the pastry wouldn't be needed. "It looks delicious." He'd eaten his share of rolls from vending machines and convenience stores. This one didn't need help.

They sat side by side, drinking their coffee, eating their rolls, reading the paper, occasionally discussing an interesting article. Twenty minutes later, Jake realized he hadn't heard a single siren the whole time. Listening for sirens was part of his nature. He could tell a police car from an ambulance within a few seconds. The total lack of their wailing was an unexpected luxury.

"I see they've hired Coach for another year," Harmony said.

"Is that a good thing?"

"Oak Grove is too small to have a decent team." She closed the sports section and laid it on the stair behind them. "We haven't had a winning season in years. But the alumni and school board don't want to give up on it. And every year, at least one boy gets a college scholarship, so they keep the team going. In a good year, two or three boys will get scholarships, even if they are to colleges no one ever heard of."

Was it possible that the entire town was as innocent as she was? Or was theirs a fantasy world that pretended people like Duane and the others at the Purple Onion didn't exist? "Wouldn't it be easier to put the money into a scholarship fund for all the kids in Oak Grove?"

"Oh, we have one of those, too. In fact, some of the money for it comes from the sales of food at the football games."

And he was about to destroy the innocence.

A stroll in the park topped off the morning. Harmony claimed that she needed to burn off all the calories from the cinnamon roll, but Jake suspected she wanted to get away from her place. His theory of why involved avoiding the bedroom and lots of sex, but that was wistful thinking. He kept up his stream of little compliments, not just of her, but the town. How clean the park was, how nice the sidewalks weren't full of cigarette butts, how even the local geese behaved themselves.

That one made her giggle.

"The city council members fight about the geese constantly," she grinned. "Half the town thinks they show how well the town is doing in preserving parks and green areas, the other half thinks they stink, their poop is messy and they don't like them chasing their dogs. Truth is, we've tried limiting their numbers, and it's too darn expensive."

As they watched the geese dive for fish in the park's little lake, he slipped his arm around her waist. She leaned into him, resting her head against his shoulder.

"I'm glad you came," she said.

He kissed the top of her head. "I tried to stay away, but can't resist you."

"You're such a flatterer."

He pulled her tighter. "You make it easy."

"Why, Jake?"

"Why what?"

"You travel all over. Big cities. Fancy places. How many women do you meet for business? Why me?"

"Because you aren't like those women. You're real."

"I always figured that's what scares men away."

"They're fools."

"And you're sweet."

He anticipated her next move. Harmony tilted her head and aimed to kiss him on the cheek. With impeccable timing, he turned so their lips met instead. He intended it to be a soft kiss, a prelude to intense kissing later, but she surprised him by turning it into more. As tightly as their mouths were pressed together, so were their bodies. He fought his own desires to restrain himself from taking it farther.

There weren't many people in this part of the park, although Jake could hear the cheerful voices of children on the playground beyond the trees. And as much as he was enjoying himself, he didn't think she wanted to shame herself if someone walked by. He pulled away after one more soft kiss.

"We can pick this up later, Angel."

Her face turned red. "That's not like me. Sorry if I embarrassed you."

He laughed. "Not me. I'm trying to preserve your

reputation but am totally in favor of taking this back to my room."

"Is that the only reason you came to see me?"

If all he wanted was sex, he had plenty of ladies available to share a bed with him. "I would love to strip your clothes off and show you how beautiful you are. But I'm happy to just spend time with you. You're more than a pretty face. You're smart and down to earth and fascinating."

It was true. He was regretting knowing about the book. It ruined the chances for this to be anything more than a job, no matter how much he cared for her.

Her gaze scorched his rotten soul as she studied his face, seeking the truth. He widened his eyes and parted his lips, trying to appear innocent. She wasn't hard to fool, to his regret.

"Let's go get lunch, Jake," she said softly.

# Chapter 12

After lunch, Jake and Harmony met up with Sarah to tour the old house. On the trip over from the real estate office, Jake reviewed what he'd learned from the TV shows about 'flipping' houses while half-listening to Sarah and Harmony chatter about people he'd never met. And didn't plan to.

The house looked as dilapidated as the first time he'd spotted it. Until he saw the inside, he wouldn't know how much potential it held. He wasn't holding his breath.

But just like Harmony, the house fascinated him. He'd talked himself into believing he could pull off this farce and make a profit. Or he'd move in, make the house the base of his operations, and talk Harmony into sharing it with him. But that wouldn't work. Too many town gossips keeping track of his comings and goings, and too much of a risk that Harmony would catch one of his many lies.

As Sarah unlocked the front door, he memorized the code she entered to release the box the realty company used to secure the door. How many other houses did it open?

"Ladies first," he said with a slight bow, holding the door open.

Harmony stepped inside. "Oh, dear. Sarah, you said the owners lived here?"

"They did," Sarah answered, following her. "They were renovating in their spare time. Why?"

Jake steeled himself for disappointment.

One wall in the front room was stripped down to the studs. Plaster torn off the wall lay in piles and half-empty boxes of nails, a stack of sheetrock, and other building supplies littered the room. At least the floor they stood on appeared to be solid, even if it was crisscrossed with dusty footprints.

"Oh dear is right, although I would have used other words. Well, they've made it easy to update the wiring," he said. "Let's check out the rest of the place."

He went first, having been in his share of old houses. Not legally, but he'd spent many nights in decaying homes when he had no money and nowhere else to get out of the weather, killing time by learning the art of picking locks from older teenagers. This house was in better condition than some of those. No graffiti decorated what remained of the walls, no drug paraphernalia lay scattered on the wooden floor, and he didn't spot any traces of fires being set to provide warmth for temporary inhabitants.

"How large is Oak Grove's homeless population?" he asked, pausing at the doorway to what may have been the parlor. The room was cluttered with broken furniture and other garbage.

"It varies by the season," Sarah said. "We have a few, but nothing like Pittsburgh. Why? Is there a problem?"

"Not that I've seen so far. But you might want to get a contractor to haul away this stuff."

Harmony peered over his shoulder. "Looks like someone had big dreams of being able to fix this and then gave up."

Jake hoped the rest of the house wasn't in the same condition. "At least they didn't tear down the walls in here." But a vague odor made him worry about the kitchen, the next room on the tour.

But the kitchen was clean. Not Harmony-clean, but cleaner than the rest of the house. Except for a few banged-up old pots, the cupboards were empty, as was the refrigerator. But the stink was stronger here, and Jake scanned the room, looking for the source.

"What do you think, Jake?" Harmony asked.

"The first step is to get a clean-up crew to make a stab at the mess. I wish I could figure out where the stench is coming from."

Sarah wrinkled her nose. "Me too."

Harmony wandered around the kitchen, sniffing. "That's odd. Even the garbage can is empty."

"If there are dead rats in the walls, it'll be a problem," he said.

"The odor is strongest here." Harmony stopped wandering and unlocked the back door.

It was a simple lock, one Jake could pick in his sleep. Nothing in the house was worth stealing, but if he ever needed a place to hide out, this would work.

She opened the door, and the stench strengthened. Sarah gagged. Jake had smelled worse, but it was bad. Harmony slammed the door shut.

"And there's the problem," she said. "They took out the garbage but left it on the back porch. Animals have been in it and it's all over the place."

Sarah rushed out of the kitchen, phone in hand. Jake followed her but went upstairs to check out the rest of the three-story house. The rooms were small, and he wondered if he'd be able to tear out walls to make them bigger. As he started up the narrow stairs to the third floor, Sarah's voice floated up to him.

"What are you doing with him, Harmony?"

"He asked me to come along."

"That's not what I mean, and you know it."

"He's good looking, smart, and treats me like I'm special. Every guy I've ever dated in Oak Grove acts as if they're doing me a favor by taking me out. They're looking for a 1950s housewife. Jake talks to me and actually listens to what I have to say."

Jake didn't want to move and make a noise that would stop the conversation. It was confirmation that his plan was working. Pride warred with a heavy dose of guilt.

"What does he want from you?"

"You mean besides the normal? Sex? Which will happen when I decide I'm ready."

Her statement was followed by a long silence, and Jake wondered if they'd gone outside. Then Harmony spoke again.

"I've asked myself the same question. And I don't have an answer. But I'm not sure it matters. He won't hang around forever, and what's wrong with having a little fun right now?"

"I don't trust him and can't tell you why, but there it is. I don't want you to get hurt, that's all."

"You want the truth? I can almost guarantee Jake will break my heart. And the fun we'll have until that happens will be worth it. I hope."

Jake shifted positions, and the stair squeaked. Time to come out of hiding. "Did I lose you two?" he called as he walked downstairs.

"We were trying to stay out of your way," Harmony said, her eyes not meeting his. A clear giveaway that she was lying. He'd have to teach her how to avoid that. "Do you like what you've seen so far?"

He very much liked what he saw, but that wasn't what she meant. He waited until he reached them to answer. "I'm worried. The asking price is too high for anyone to make a profit from remodeling. The value is in the land. I can see a developer buying the house but tearing it down and putting up a small apartment complex."

"The Historical Society will fight that," Sarah said.

"The legal costs will make it unprofitable. Will the historical group require a restoration instead of bringing it up to modern standards?"

Sarah frowned. "With other houses, they've been satisfied by preserving the character of the house, if not every detail."

"It's a gamble." Jake crossed his arms. "I'd have to see what local contractors are charging for the major jobs. The house appeals to me, but I haven't even checked out the roof or the heating system." He hoped he sounded like he knew what he was talking about.

"The roof was replaced five years ago, according to the paperwork," Sarah said.

"Good to know." Jake used his phone to take a series of pictures, mostly of the damage in the front room. "Any other maintenance records you can find will help. Was there an inspection done when the owners bought the place? How open are they to negotiating the price?"

"The ex-husband wants to dump it and run. The ex-wife is positive the house is a goldmine. She's already called the agency and complained that no one has made an offer yet." Sarah's lips curled. "My boss tried to tell her she's dreaming but hasn't convinced her. He thinks a few bids at rock-bottom price will help her face reality."

They'd walked outside while they were talking. Jake stopped to give the house one more glance. "I'm surprised the city hasn't condemned it," he said.

"The code enforcement department is so far behind, it'll be weeks before they ever come out to look. That will give a buyer a chance to get the proper permits to fix it," Sarah said.

"Harmony, what do you think?" Jake asked.

"Can you imagine how this looked when it was first built?" Her eyes lost their focus. "And what it must have been like to live here? Back when the women wore long, flowing dresses and fancy hats? And the men wore morning coats and top hats? Roses in bloom would fill the garden and flower baskets would line the steps leading inside."

Sarah grinned. "Did Harmony tell you she's a history freak?"

"She did." Jake's mouth twitched. "That's how we

met." A lie, but close to the truth, it slipped easily from his lips.

"Are you laughing at me?" Harmony gently punched Jake's shoulder.

"Absolutely not. I'm admiring your beautiful brain."

"He's good." Sarah chuckled.

"And now I'm going to have to factor in how happy it will make Harmony into my budget." Jake pretended to draw numbers and do math in the air. "Or I can decrease costs by wrangling her into helping me with painting. Or hauling away the garbage." He added more scribbles to his imaginary calculations.

"The firm is going to handle that," Sarah said. "I spoke to my boss. We'll just add the cost to the fees. We don't want to attract mice."

Jake gave the house one last look before opening the car door for Harmony. Could he do this? Not as part of his plot to get the book, but to establish his persona as a successful contractor? What doors would that open for him in other parts of his life?

✿ ✿ ✿

"You're quiet tonight," Harmony said.

Jake twisted spaghetti around his fork. They were eating supper at Mama D's again, but hadn't gotten the back booth this time. Still, people weren't interrupting their meal, and the service was excellent, as always. "Sorry, I was thinking about the house," Jake answered.

"It's in terrible shape, isn't it?"

"Yes. At least the structure looks sound, but I'd want

a second opinion on that. We didn't even go into the basement, and who knows what's down there?"

"Is it worth fixing?"

Jake exhaled loudly. "That's the question."

"Don't do this for me, Jake. It needs to be a business decision, nothing more."

He reached across the table and covered her hand with his. "I keep imagining how great it would be to bring the house back to life."

"It got to you, didn't it?"

"Like you got to me." One side of his mouth lifted. "I didn't expect it to happen."

She shook her head. "There you go again, saying the sweetest things and being hard to resist."

He arched his eyebrow and twirled the end of a non-existent handlebar mustache. "Part of my evil plot to get you into my bed."

"You keep it up and your wish may come true." She fluttered her eyelashes.

He'd been propositioned many times and knew how to control his body's reaction. That was forgotten. "Your place or mine?" he asked, putting down his fork and using his other hand to discretely adjust himself under the table.

"Finish your supper, Jake," she said. "We can decide the details later. Anticipation is part of the fun."

She was going to make him crazy. But he hoped to enjoy every minute.


Supper dragged on forever and Jake suspected she

was delaying the inevitable. Whether from nervousness or toying with him, he wasn't sure. Perhaps she wasn't as naive as he'd assumed. They ended up going back to her place so she could put her leftovers in the fridge. That was the reason she gave, anyway. Jake couldn't figure her out. Did she feel safe there and in control? Or was she hiding a dark secret she'd spring on him at the last moment? He was supposed to be in charge, and Little Miss Innocent had turned the tables.

While she fussed in the kitchen, he studied the bookshelves again. Still no sign of The Three Musketeers.

"Find something interesting?" she asked, coming out of the kitchen carrying a tray with two cups of coffee, a bowl of sugar, and powdered creamer.

He rushed to assist her. "You own quite the collection. I wondered which book you'd assign me next."

She set the cups on the coffee table, making sure each had a coaster centered under it. "You choose this time."

"I get to challenge you to something first, if I remember correctly."

"And I have veto power."

Damn, he'd forgotten that. So much for his plan of having her do a striptease in the front room. "I'm still thinking." He wrapped his arm around her waist. "How about a kiss for inspiration?"

# Chapter 13

"A kiss for inspiration? Nothing else? You're selling yourself short, Jake," Harmony said as she laid her hand on his chest.

Jake blinked. "I never know where I stand with you, Angel."

She grasped his collar and tugged. A captive to her eyes, he went willingly, bending to meet her lips with his. Desire scorched every muscle in his body. She took the lead, running her tongue over his lips, until he could no longer resist and mashed their mouths together.

"Angel," he groaned as she ran a soft hand down his chest.

With no warning, she pulled away. "Is that enough inspiration?"

His definition of inspired and hers were two different things. "Tomorrow, I'll take you out to that abandoned road and teach you how to do a J-turn."

"What's a J-turn?"

He wasn't above teasing her. "Let's just say James Bond would approve of it."

She bit her bottom lip. "I wonder if I can torture the secret out of you."

What did she have in mind? Jake couldn't wait to find out.

Her opening move was to trace a line from his forehead to the tip of his nose, then to his lips. Sweet, but not torture. The finger kept moving. She ran it down his neck and to the first button on his shirt. He grabbed her hand, but she pushed his away and grinned. "Play along, Jake. Or are you ready to give up and tell me your secrets yet?"

"You need to do better than that," he warned her. He'd have to be on guard.

She released the button from its hole, moved onto the second, then stopped and started at the top again. Only this time, when she reached his lips, she kissed him, then continued tracing her finger down his chest. The third and fourth buttons fell victim to her efforts, and he wondered how far she'd take things.

Her finger moved back to his forehead, and he planned for the moment of the kiss. It didn't happen. Instead, her lips touched the spot where the first button had been, then the second, followed by the finger moving farther south.

Jake was a patient man when he needed to be. She was testing his limits.

Harmony unbuttoned the fifth button and pulled his shirt out of the waistband of his pants. He swallowed hard. How far would she go to prove her point? She freed the last button and pushed his shirt to the sides and bared his chest. Her hands brushed across his nipples before they moved lower. His breathing sped up, and there wasn't a way to hide the bulge in his pants. He clasped his hands behind his back, letting her play.

"Tell me what a J-turn is," she said as she kissed the bare skin just above his belt buckle.

"No," he moaned.

She undid the buckle, then reached up and started tracing the same path from his forehead. "Tell me, Jake."

"No."

She stopped, leaving her finger on the tip of his nose. "Last chance."

He didn't dare break the spell by wiping the sweat beads from his forehead. "Or what?"

She placed her lips on his, then pulled his shirt together and started the slow process of fastening each button.

Jake broke. He grabbed her hands and pulled them behind his back. "It's a way to turn around quickly. You start by going fast in reverse, brake, clutch and turn the steering wheel at the same time. You end up heading in the opposite direction." He lowered his head and smashed his lips into hers. She didn't object.

He reached to slide the pins out of her bun, but she pulled away.

"I accept the challenge," she said. "But the coffee is probably cold by now. Do you want me to make more?"

"Where the hell did you learn to do that?" he asked, trying to catch his breath.

She grinned. "I read it in a book. Although the heroine took it further. She got the guy's pants off."

"What happened next?"

"If I remember correctly, she put a sleeping potion in the spy's coffee and slipped away."

Jake gulped, picked up his cup, and swirled the liquid in it, searching for traces of something that didn't belong.

Harmony winked, took the coffee from his hands, sipped it, frowned, and wrinkled her nose. "Yep, cold."

However slick he thought he was, he was no match for her. "I don't want coffee," he said, his voice rough.

"What do you want, Jake?"

Did he detect longing in her voice? "You. I want to taste every inch of you. Then I want to start over again. And when neither of us can stand it any longer, I want to make love to you."

"What's stopping you?"

Those were the words he'd been waiting to hear.

❄ ❄ ❄

He sat on the edge of her bed, trying to figure out the protocol for the situation while he waited for her to come out of the bathroom. He wanted to stay and hold her for the rest of the night, but he'd never known anyone like her. What did she expect?

She'd been the perfect lover. Matching his every move, giving as much as she took. He was exhausted, but ready for more. Later. They both needed time to recuperate.

The bookshelf was in front of him and, out of habit, he scanned the titles. There it was, on the top shelf. The Three Musketeers. He pulled the book off the shelf and flipped through the pages. He'd heard of the story, but the archaic language wasn't something he'd be comfortable reading.

"Find your next book?" Harmony asked from the doorway. She'd slipped on a t-shirt and panties.

Jake felt at a disadvantage. He hadn't even found his shorts yet. "I don't think so."

She sat on the bed beside him and took the book from his hands. "It's a classic. You should try an updated edition."

"Have you read this one?" Silly question, but he was at a loss for words. The book was worth thousands, and she treated it like any other.

"Lots. I received it as a birthday present when I was twelve and I've had it all these years. It was my Uncle Loren's. He picked it up in England when he was in the military. It's old, but it isn't a first edition or anything, so it's only worth a few bucks. Except to me, it's priceless."

Everything he'd worked towards for the last few months shattered, falling in shards to the floor.

"I had a newspaper reporter ask about it once. There was a rumor that I had an 1846 version. I don't know how it got started. Anyway, I ruined her day when I showed her this. I've got plenty of old books, but nothing in the price range she hoped to include in her article."

At least he wasn't the first one to fall for the falsehood.

She gathered her waist-long hair and twisted it into a loose bun. He stared in fascination as all that hair disappeared into a messy bundle and was struck with the desire to let it fall free again. But he was seemingly glued to the bed and unable to move.

"Do you want something to drink?" she asked, placing the book on the shelf.

"I could go for a glass of cold water," he said. A shot of whiskey would be better, but he hadn't spotted any hard liquor in her cupboards.

As soon as she left, he rustled through the sheets until he found his shorts. He didn't understand why, but he was uncomfortable walking around naked in her apartment. He slipped them on, then paused and picked up the book again. To verify what she'd told him, he flipped to the opening pages. The copyright was dated 1955, so this wasn't the valuable antique he'd hoped to find.

The cloud of guilt he'd been living with lifted as he walked down the short hallway to her kitchen. His disappointment in not getting the book drifted away. He'd proven he could have made off with the volume if it had existed, satisfying his ego. And there was a lovely lady with a glass of cold water in her hand coming his way. She satisfied him in a different way.

❈ ❈ ❈

Jake woke to the scent of coffee and a bed without Harmony in it. After a quick stop in the bathroom, he went to the kitchen expecting to find her, but she wasn't there. She must be reading her paper on her steps. He couldn't join her without getting dressed, which led back to the bathroom and a quick shower. She'd even laid out a towel for him.

After pouring himself a cup of coffee, he scavenged through her cupboards to find where she kept the dog treats. He didn't want to go empty-handed. Even if he never expected to sneak back into her place, it always paid off to stay friends with the dog.

"Good morning," he called as he bounced down the stairs. When he reached the bottom, he kissed Harmony on the forehead before tossing the treat to the pooch and sitting beside her. "Anything interesting in the paper today?"

"A pawnshop was robbed yesterday." She handed him the front page. "Not my favorite, but I've been there."

"Do you go to pawnshops often?"

"That's where I get a lot of my books."

Jake scanned the article. There weren't many details, but it appeared to be another smash and grab scenario. He didn't like it. It seemed he was being followed. At least he had an alibi. He wondered what Carl at the Purple Onion knew.

"Probably a druggie looking for a quick way to get money for their next fix," he said. "Do me a favor and stay away until the cops catch the guy. I don't want you caught in the middle of trouble."

She patted his knee. "I promise I'll be careful."

He'd have to live with that for now.


After a trip to the motel for a change of clothes, Jake felt more presentable. He gassed up the Charger on the way back to Harmony's, hoping to take her out driving. He looked forward to teaching her the J-turn maneuver.

First, he made a stop at the Purple Onion. As he expected, it was open for business. Carl wasn't behind the bar, but Jake got his whiskey, overpaid for it, and found a seat in the corner. He knew how things worked.

Word would get to Carl about the stranger, along with a picture snapped on the bartender's cell phone. If Carl had any information to pass along, Jake would get an invitation to the office. How much information depended on how much cash he paid for his next drink.

He nursed the whiskey for as long as possible. Long enough that if he stayed too much longer, Harmony might get worried. He hadn't told her about the side trip. He decided nothing was going to happen and stood to leave.

"Leaving so soon?" Carl asked from the back hallway. "I didn't think we'd see you today."

"I didn't expect to be here."

"Wanna join me for a drink?"

The eyes of the other customers trailed Jake as he followed Carl. He ignored the tingle that spoke of danger. The setup was a test he had to pass.

They sat on opposite sides of Carl's desk. "What's bothering you?" Carl poured a shot of whiskey into a tumbler and shoved it towards Jake. He already had a glass sitting on his side.

Jake paid for both shots, along with an extra ten. "The pawnshop robbery wasn't the work of a local, was it?"

Carl tensed. "Fuck. You are a cop."

"No." Jake sipped his drink. "I think someone is sending me a message. I don't want anyone here to get hurt."

"Especially one little librarian?"

"Especially her."

"She's a nice lady. She smiles at me when I go to the library. Never acts likes she's better than the rest of us because of her money. The others ignore me."

*Harmony? Money?* Jake swallowed his astonishment with a deep swallow of his whiskey. What money? He couldn't ask any of the questions that jumbled around in his brain.

"Who's looking for you?" Carl asked.

Jake pulled himself together. "The better question is which side of the law they are on. And if they are my friend or my enemy."

"And?"

"It could be either."

"What do you want from me?"

Jake put two twenties on the desk. "Nothing. I don't want to get anyone else involved. But if there's a way I can protect my friends, let me know."

"Are you planning on sticking around?"

"I'm leaving tomorrow morning."

"That's not much time."

Jake grimaced. "I have other commitments. And I'm hoping when I leave, so will the other guy. But there's no way for me to be sure."

"You've got a problem, all right."

"Yeah."

Carl downed the rest of his whiskey and poured himself another. Jake laid another twenty on the desk to pay for it.

"We open at eight," Carl said. "If you have a chance to drop by before you hit the road, come say hi."

Jake finished his drink in one swallow. "Thanks."

# Chapter 14

Jake hadn't expected Harmony to be such a good student, with nerves of steel. She didn't scream when he demonstrated the J-turn—going fast in reverse, braking, clutching and turning the steering wheel at the same time—with her in the passenger's seat. Instead, she'd asked him to repeat the maneuver so she could study his movements. When he'd instructed her to drive in reverse as fast as possible, she'd gone fast enough that he clutched the dashboard.

On her first attempt, she hadn't mashed the brakes hard enough. The second time, she got the brakes right and the yank on the steering wheel wrong. She missed the shift and killed the engine twice. Now, she'd made all the right moves three in a row.

She had her hands on the wheel and the biggest grin ever on her face. "Can I do it again?"

"Nope. That's it for today. Too much, and you'll get tired and sloppy. Besides, what we are doing is in the gray area between legal and illegal and the longer we stay, the bigger the chance a cop will show up."

"What law are we breaking? Besides the speed limit?"

Which she'd likely broken going in reverse. "The easiest would be exhibition driving. This is a public road, even if no one uses it."

"I can see some old farmer calling the Highway Patrol on us." The car was in neutral, her left foot was on the brake, and she used her right to rev the engine. "I don't suppose I should try this in George."

"Not unless you plan to buy a new car."

She shook her head. "That's not in the budget. I need to keep George running as long as possible. Now what?"

So, Carl was mistaken. Harmony didn't have money. A bit of information the Oak Grove rumor mill got wrong.

"Let's get lunch." Jake rubbed his stomach. "I'm hungry after all that exercise last night and skipping breakfast. But let's not go back to Oak Grove. What's north of here?"

"I don't know. I haven't been this way in forever. Let's find out." As gently as a feather, she pushed in the clutch and shifted into first. She didn't even ask to drive.

Jake hid his grin. So much for the quiet little librarian. He liked this new version of Harmony.


They ate lunch at a chain restaurant near Edinboro. Afterward, Jake insisted on taking over driving duties. His excuse was that it was his turn, but his gut warned of more. He stuck to the interstate and the speed limit, obeying every traffic law. A state trooper passed them in the opposite lane, but Jake didn't see any cause for alarm. Still, worry gnawed at him.

Halfway home, they got caught behind two semis traveling side-by-side. Not an unusual occurrence, but these two seemed to be in a competition. Or they were in a duel. At each little hill, the one on the left would pull ahead. On each downgrade, the one on the right would catch up and get in front. They both ignored the traffic building up behind them.

Jake backed off, letting other cars pass. "Is there an exit we can take to get off this road, Angel?" he asked as he braked to avoid a car cutting in front of him.

"I'm not familiar with this road," she answered. "And I'm not seeing anything on my maps app."

That didn't help. He rotated his shoulders to ease the tension. Beside them, a car zoomed by in the emergency pull-off strip on the right-hand side of the road.

"Shit," he cursed, refraining from stronger words. He braked and dropped down a gear.

Neither of the trucks held a straight line as they were buffeted by their tailwinds. They swayed and rocked, but the trailers didn't meet. Jake prayed for a third lane to open before disaster struck.

The squealing of brakes and blaring of horns were signs of what was to come. The grass alongside the road was the only safe place to go. He yanked the steering wheel to the right. The Charger's tires bucked in the uneven dirt, sending up dust clouds. Jake clung to the wheel, mashed on the brakes, and brought the car to a stop. He took a deep breath and turned off the engine.

Harmony wrestled with the latch on her seatbelt. Jake loosened his grip and put out his hand to stop her. "Wait."

"We have to help."

The screech of metal against metal was followed by a car spinning out of control, coming to rest a few feet behind them. Ahead, two cars careened into each other. Jake placed a calming hand on her shoulder. "We will, when it's safe. Do you know first aid?"

She nodded. "We had a course at the library."

"Good, because I know nothing." He rolled down his window to listen. No sirens, but plenty of people crying, horns honking, engines sputtering. "We'll give it another minute to be on the safe side."

He should have kept his eye on her. She had her door open when he turned back around.

"I'm not waiting. Are you coming?"

If he wanted to protect her, he didn't have a choice. He followed her to a car that had slid by and stood guard as she ran through a list of questions. Satisfied that none of the three people in the car were badly hurt, she moved on to the next one.

By then, sirens echoed in the distance. Professionals were on the way. He hoped they'd get there before she came across anyone seriously injured. How would she handle the sight of blood pouring from a head wound?

It wasn't hard to direct her towards the back of the pack, where he expected the injuries to be less severe. She'd check out bumps and bruises and calmed the fears of the scared. He hung in the background, watching for gas leaking from wrecked vehicles, telling people to turn off their engines, and clearing broken glass so people wouldn't get cut.

"Jake," Harmony called from a few cars away. "Come help me."

"What do you need?"

"I can't get the back door open."

The door was dented, but not crushed, and Jake didn't have to ask why she wanted to open it. A baby was strapped in the car seat in the back, whimpering but not crying. However, the mother, in the front seat, was frantic to get to her child. Her door had taken more damage, and it would take professional tools to open it. Not that the mother should get out, anyway. The window was down, and Harmony had wrapped a scarf or something around the mother's neck so she couldn't move it, more as a precaution than based on any visual injury. The front door on the passenger's side wiggled when he yanked on it but didn't give. He tugged on the back door on the passenger's side, but it wouldn't budge, even though it was unlocked. He considered breaking the glass in the window, but he didn't want it to shatter onto the infant. The rear window looked to be his best option. If he broke it and cleaned out the glass, he'd be able to crawl into the back seat. All he needed was a heavy-duty screwdriver. Or a tire iron.

"Angel," he said, "ask the lady for her keys. I want to open the trunk." That was another way, although he didn't think he'd be able to squirm through the trunk to the back seat in the compact car.

She tossed the keys to him, and he snatched them out of the air. The rear end wasn't damaged, and it opened with only minor creaking. He dug through layers of baby equipment to get to the spare tire.

The baby was quiet, and Jake worried it was injured. Either that or it had worn itself out and fallen asleep.

"What's the baby's name?" he asked. He unscrewed the clamp that held the tire and jack in place.

In a soothing tone, Harmony spoke to the mother. "Jenny," she said to Jake. "The baby's name is Jenny."

He nodded. "Tell the mother I'm going to break the glass. Let her know I'll be careful not to hurt Jenny."

"Got it," she said, and resumed talking to the mother.

The trick was to hit in the corner of the glass, not the middle. He felt it give under the first whack, but not break. He adjusted his aim and tried again. The window was tougher than he expected. He tightened his grip and brought the tire iron down with every bit of strength he could summon. His reward was a satisfying crunch and a hole in the glass.

A tattered blanket from the trunk provided the protection he needed to clean out remnants of glass from the window frame, making a spot big enough for him to wiggle through. He climbed onto the car and slid, feet first, into the back seat.

"Hey, Jenny," he said to the baby, who looked at him with wide, black eyes. "Let's get you out of here." He wondered if there was a way to get the entire baby seat out of the car. He was good at locks, but he'd never touched a contraption like this. "How does this work, ma'am?"

"You take the seat out of the base," she said.

Jake was lost but figured undoing the seat belt was a good start.

"It's two pieces," the lady said. "Don't undo the straps holding her in. There's a latch on the front."

His presence in the car seemed to comfort her, and her crying slowed. Jake felt around and found the mechanism she was talking about. It clicked when he pushed the button. The seat came out, baby and all.

"Hey, little Jenny," he said. "Angel, come to the back window, and I'll pass her through."

It worked. Jake tossed another bag containing baby supplies through the opening, then maneuvered himself out of the car.

Harmony was by the driver's window, showing Jenny to her mother, and cooing to the little one. He wondered if she wanted kids because he sure didn't.

A paramedic, carrying his bag of equipment, ran up. "Everyone all right here?" the paramedic asked.

Jake stood back while Harmony explained the situation. His job was complete, at least for this little family.


By the time they made it back to Oak Grove. Jake wasn't hungry, but knew they both needed to eat. "Feel like grabbing a burger and taking it to your place?"

They'd left without giving their names to the authorities. The Charger had been undamaged, and once the highway patrol took charge of the scene, he'd driven in the grass to the next exit a mile up the road. He preferred to remain anonymous.

"What I want to do," Harmony answered, "is make a cup of tea and sit on my couch and read. Maybe take a hot bath and soak until the water goes cold. I don't have the energy for more than that."

"I hear you." Truth was, he wasn't up to a repeat of the previous night's performance. But he'd exchange the cup of tea for a stiff drink or three and the book for the senseless drone of whatever was on TV. Or he could find a connection at the Purple Onion to sell him a joint. But that wasn't worth the risk.

They rode in silence the rest of the way to her place. He parked, turned off the car, and unbuckled his seatbelt while she unbuckled hers.

"Jake," she said, weariness coloring her voice.

"No worries, Angel, I'll just make sure you get to your door safely." If he got a goodnight kiss at the top, that would be enough.

She didn't move, and he wondered what was going on in her head. As hard as he tried, he couldn't read her.

"Thank you for today," she said after a long pause. She opened her car door. "It was fun until that whole major disaster part. Will you swing by and say goodbye before you leave tomorrow?"

*Willingly.* "I can do that."

They walked in silence up the stairs. After unlocking and opening her door, she turned and put a hand on his chest. "We made a good team today, didn't we?"

"You did the hard work. Talking to people and checking them out."

"But you rescued little Jenny. I wouldn't have known what to do."

He knew a lot about breaking into things. This time there'd been a different reward. "I didn't even know how to undo the baby seat."

The corners of her lips curled. "Me neither. Despite what everyone assumes, not all women are experts in raising children."

Jake couldn't help himself. He wrapped his arms around her, pulling her head to his shoulder. "We do make a good team."

She leaned into him. They stood there for what seemed like forever, but not long enough.

She finally stepped back. "Good night, Jake," she said, raising her chin.

He took it as an invitation and brought his head down to hers. Their lips met, and a spark of longing blossomed in Jake's veins. He didn't act on it, but let his mouth linger. "Good night," he said as he straightened.

He waited as she went inside and closed the door. Jake listened but didn't hear a mechanical click. "Lock your door, Angel," he called, then trekked back to his car.


Once he was back in his motel room, Jake turned on the little TV. It was set to a news channel out of Pittsburgh, and he didn't bother changing it. The cute blonde news anchor smiled as she showed film from the accident. He poured himself a whiskey and sat on the end of the bed to watch the pictures flash by.

One truck had tipped over, spilling its load of paper goods and causing the chain of crashes. "At least they had what they needed for cleaning," Jake murmured as a paramedic scooped up several rolls of paper towels. The focus of the report was the worst of the damage and he didn't glimpse Harmony, the Charger, or himself. Good. He preferred it that way.

# Chapter 15

The Purple Onion only had three customers when Jake showed up mid-morning. The daytime bartender, Danny, poured him a shot. Jake took it to the table in the back corner, to hide from the stares of the other men. What had changed?

It didn't take long for Carl to join him. Except this time, Carl sat with him and brought a bottle of whiskey. Not the standard way of doing business.

Carl grinned and raised his glass in a salute. "So, you're a celebrity now."

"What are you talking about?"

"You made the news, hero."

*It must have been on a different channel.* Jake took a deep swallow of his whiskey. "Damn."

"Saving a baby? So much for keeping a low profile."

"I didn't leave my name, so I guess I'm covered." Jake put his hand over his glass when Carl went to refill it. "I have a long drive ahead of me."

Carl topped off his own glass. Jake, playing by the rules, laid a twenty on the table. Carl pushed the money back at him. "Not today. You helped the friend of a friend. But unfortunately, I can't help you with your problem. No one knows anything about the pawn shop robberies."

"It was worth a try." Jake left the money where it lay and stood. "I'll drop by the next time I'm in town."

Carl nodded and pocketed the twenty. By the time Jake hit the front door and glanced back, the table was empty.

❄ ❄ ❄

He had another stop to make on his way out of town. First, he bought a package of breath mints at a convenience store and used the store's restroom to change his shirt before heading to the library. His double life took a lot of work.

From inside the library's front door, he watched Harmony help an old lady check out a stack of books and slip them into a canvas bag. The bag appeared to be too heavy for the woman, and even her cane didn't steady her as she struggled to walk to the door.

Harmony rushed to assist her, but Jake got there first.

"Let me help you," he said, crooking his arm and offering it to the elderly lady.

"Do I know you?" she asked. "Well, guess it doesn't matter. Here, take this." She shoved the bag at Jake.

He took the bag as the old woman grabbed his arm, then looked up to see Harmony laughing at him.

"Mrs. Buford's ride is on the way," she grinned. "They're picking her up at the bus stop."

Not that Jake had much of a choice at that point. He waved at Harmony, held the door for Mrs. Buford, and let her cling to him as she hobbled down the stairs, chattering about her granddaughter and how pretty she was, and did he want to meet her because they'd make beautiful babies. She kept rambling about grandchildren and great grandchildren as she settled on the bench.

He handed her the books, realized that she'd never stop talking, and said, "I have to run," and did, all the way back inside.

Harmony was still laughing as she met him at the door. "I think Mrs. Buford likes you."

"She's sweet, but does she ever run out of breath?" Jake asked.

"Depends. Today, not so much. What are you doing here? I figured you were on your way home."

"You don't think I'd leave without saying goodbye, do you?" Jake winked. "I wish I could do it properly, but that might get you fired."

Her cheeks turned dark red. "Drive safe. After yesterday, I'll worry about you."

"I'll be fine." He wanted to hug her, but people were looking.

She hesitated, then grabbed his hand. "Come with me."

He didn't know what she was up to but followed willingly. She led him to a doorway and steps that went downstairs. "No one ever uses these," she said. "But we only have a minute. Kiss me, quick."

He wanted to take it slow. It would have to last him for too long. But she'd asked, so he'd give her what she requested. A short kiss, but one that would make her wish for more. The problem was, he left wishing for more, too.

❀ ❀ ❀

There were two shadows across the street from Shaggy's, but Jake was too busy to talk to Alex and whoever her friend was. The men at the night's bachelor party didn't understand that the servers weren't part of the entertainment, and he and Marty stayed occupied keeping things under control. That and making sure the three guys they'd tossed out didn't sneak back in.

It was one in the morning before business slowed down and Jake had time to talk about anything besides work. Marty brought the observers up first.

"You notice we have double trouble watching us?" he asked.

"Yep. Were they there while I was off?"

"Not that I noticed."

Well, at least Alex kept her promise. "I've got a confession. Remember how I took off early last week?"

"Yeah?"

"When the bar closed, I followed the shadow. Right to where they live. Caught him sneaking into an apartment. We had a long talk."

"Rough him up, did you?" Marty chuckled. "And now they're back with reinforcements?"

"Nope. We actually talked. Turns out he's a she. Her name is Alex."

Marty sucked in a noisy breath. "How old is this Alex?"

"I didn't ask. Thirteen, fourteen, I guess?"

"What does she want?"

Marty stared across the street and Jake couldn't see his face, but he suspected Marty knew the answer. "She seems to think you're her father."

"Cover me." Without waiting for Jake to agree, Marty took off.

Jake didn't have time to track what happened, because yelling from inside the bar demanded his presence. Once the bachelor group left to continue their party in another type of establishment, the bartender told him Marty had clocked out for the night. Some kind of family emergency. Jake hoped things had worked out for Alex.

※ ※ ※

The newspapers that Jake accessed through the Atlanta libraries hadn't given him any leads to jobs for weeks. No society weddings, major classical music events, or openings for big art shows. His fingers itched for a big score, but he was playing it safe. He needed a new challenge and a new market for passing on his loot. One where the smash-and-grab robber wouldn't follow him.

He hadn't heard of any more thefts since his return. The Pittsburgh news was quiet, too. Marty hadn't reported anyone lurking near the bar, but that didn't mean they weren't there.

He needed a job on the West Coast. Or Texas. With all the oil money there, someone had to have cash to throw around for unique jewels. He'd given up on the jewelry exhibit at the historical site. He had a rule against doing jobs too close to home and Oak Grove counted as a second home.

Harmony had called multiple times to find out when he was coming back. All he could tell her was soon. First, he had to figure out how to get the money to buy the house. Sarah kept working on the owners to get the price reduced, but it wasn't low enough yet. Not with the repairs it needed.

A visit to the zoo would take his mind off things. Even if the opportunity to steal a random jewel didn't arise, an afternoon of people watching would entertain him.

❋ ❋ ❋

"Grandma, let's go see the goats," the little brown-haired boy said, tugging on her sleeve.

Jake hadn't figured out why grandma had come on this trip. She only seemed interested in her phone and didn't pay any attention to her grandson.

Mom shook her head and pointed to a nearby exhibit. "Want to feed the giraffes, Drew? We can go see the goats later."

The little boy's lip trembled. "That's what you said last time. And we never go'ed."

"Goats belong on a farm," Grandma said. "That's not why we come to the zoo."

Jake hated her. He couldn't do anything to help Drew, but he could punish Grandma in his own way.

The diamond earrings she wore didn't belong at the zoo. Wouldn't it be a shame if at least one of them fell off and got trampled? If they were clip-ons, he would make that happen. Pierced earrings were more of a challenge, but still only a matter of a little sleight-of-hand.

He waited to make his move until they reached the lion exhibit. Drew seemed to be interested in them, and he and mom left grandma behind on the sidewalk when they walked up to the fence to get a better view. Jake pulled out his phone, brought up the zoo's map, and headed towards the warthogs. He knocked into Grandma and dropped his phone.

"Oh my, I am so sorry," he said, and reached out to help the woman regain her balance. "I wasn't watching where I was going."

"You should be careful," she snapped.

"You're absolutely right." He bent to pick up his phone, and on the way up, stumbled and banged into her again.

"What's wrong with you!" She pushed him away.

Jake blinked rapidly. "That's better. It's these new contacts. I can't get them to sit right on my eyes. They have me all off balance. At least I bumped into a pretty lady instead of a cranky old man. I am so sorry. Can I buy you a soda as an apology?"

She hesitated, then waved in the direction of the boy and his mother. "My family..."

"Is that your sister and nephew? They're welcome to join us."

She giggled.

Jake couldn't believe she was buying the nonsense

he spouted. "I think the little boy looks more like you than his mother," he continued.

"They're busy. We won't bother them." She put her hand on Jake's arm. "Do you need me to guide you to the refreshment stand?"

She was making this too easy. He had an earring in his pocket before he even paid for the drinks; snagged when he 'tripped' over an uneven spot in the sidewalk and she helped him get back up. But with all the security cameras, he wouldn't press his luck and go for two. The diamonds appeared to be second-rate stones, anyway. At least, the one he'd snagged had a cloudy flaw. She'd probably bought them from one of those TV shows that made big promises but sold junk.

His real reward was that Drew and his mother got to pet the goats while he sat on a bench, drank a soda, and flirted with the old lady, who lapped up every lie and slipped him her phone number. The one he gave her in return was for a strip joint outside city limits.

Grandma slurped the last bit of her drink. "I guess I should catch up with the baby," she said with a heavy, fake sigh.

Drew, the baby, was at least 5 years old. "I'm sure they're missing you."

"I don't know why we even bother coming here. All he wants to do is pet the goats. But at least I get to visit him."

*If you counted talking to a stranger in a different part of the zoo as seeing your grandchild, Jake thought as he stood.* "Enjoy the rest of your day. It was nice to meet you."

"Are you going to be okay, Ryan?"

Fake name, of course. "My eyes have finally adjusted. I'll be fine." He held out his hand for a shake, avoiding the hug she'd inevitably offer. His ploy worked, and soon she was toddling on her high heels down the path towards the goat display.

He stuck around the African exhibit, studying the pride of lions. Leaving right away would make him look suspicious if the security tapes were reviewed. It also reduced the chances he'd run into Grandma again. He wouldn't get much for the earring from his favorite fence, but he'd had fun.

Did Harmony own any 'good' jewelry? All he'd ever seen her wear was the same turquoise necklace and a small pair of gold earrings. She deserved something better. He wouldn't gift her with anything stolen, but he knew where to find a deal.

# Chapter 16

Jake signed the papers with a flourish. Across the table in the bank's conference room sat the two lawyers representing the divorced, previous owners. In the biggest scam of his career, he was now the owner of a dilapidated home in Oak Grove. Well, his fake company was. He no longer had to create excuses to be in town and visit Harmony.

Tonight, she'd be his guest for his private celebration. He patted the pocket holding a pair of legally bought, gold, dangly earrings. They'd start with dinner at The Grove, the fanciest restaurant around. With her, what followed was never a given, but he had high hopes.

The profit from a string of pearls he'd 'found by the side of the road' in San Diego was financing the celebration. Harmony thought he'd been in Billings for a conference. At least, that's where the postcard he sent her originated.

Jake had two hours to kill before he picked her up for dinner, time enough for a quick stop on the wrong side of town. He wanted to show his face at the Purple

Onion so that Carl would know he was around. It didn't hurt to keep on the good side of whatever allies he could get.

Traffic was lighter than normal, and he made it to the bar in no time flat. The front door squeaked as he pushed it open, working better than any bell to alert the entire bar of a new arrival. The regulars no longer paid attention to him when he entered. The daytime bartender nodded and had a whiskey ready by the time Jake reached the counter.

He overpaid and carried the glass to the back. Not to his usual table—because a young couple, looking out-of-place sat there—but to one on the other side of the room. If Carl had any news, he'd make an appearance. The first few swallows went down easier than usual, and Jake suspected the booze hadn't been poured from the standard bottle.

"You need a refill?" the bartender asked, swiping spilled beer and pretzel crumbs from a nearby table.

That's not the way it worked. "Thanks, but no thanks. I have a meeting in an hour."

"Carl wants to see you. You know your way?"

"I do." Jake picked up the glass holding the dregs of his drink. "Thanks."

He knocked on the office door, but didn't wait for an answer before going in. Carl was at his desk, and a man with short, gray hair sat in the corner behind him. Carl didn't introduce him.

"I need a favor," Carl said, as Jake slid into a chair. "Call it bodyguard services."

Straight to the point. This was the moment where

Jake had the opportunity to repay the favors Carl had done for him and add another notch to his reputation in Oak Grove. Or destroy it altogether. This had all the hallmarks of a test, and Jake had cheated his way through school.

"I don't carry," he pointed out.

"But I do," the other man said. "I need a set of eyes and someone who can make a quick assessment of the situation for a delivery I'm making. Driving skills are a bonus. Carl recommended you."

Jake studied the man. Slight build, medium height, a black suit that was department store variety. Not organized crime.

"It isn't anything illegal," Carl said, confirming Jake's hunch.

"I can help. Depending on when and how long." Jake trusted Carl, for the most part. But what business did anyone in Oak Grove have that required a bodyguard?

"Tomorrow. Just to Erie and back. My regular driver is sick."

Nobody offered the man's name, and Jake didn't ask. "That'll work, if it's not too early in the morning. I'm hoping for a long night tonight."

"You seeing the librarian?" Carl asked.

"Yes. But she works tomorrow, so my day is free." He turned to the unnamed man. "Will we be using my car or yours? Mine may stand out too much for your purposes."

"Yours is the bright yellow one I've seen around town?"

Jake nodded.

"I'd like to take it for a spin," the man said, "but not tomorrow. I'll send you a text in the morning with the information of where to meet."

Jake took a business card out of his wallet. He'd set up a virtual number that forwarded to his cell phone. "You can reach me here. I won't answer right away but will get back to you within a few minutes."

"You were spot on, Carl. He's good." The man grinned at Jake. "But you haven't asked about compensation."

"I assume you'll pay based on your satisfaction with how well I perform."

"Correct. Can I buy you a drink to seal the deal?"

If they played by the rules, Jake would have to accept the alcohol. Carl interrupted. "I suspect he wants a clear head for his date tonight."

Jake chuckled. "The lady keeps me on my toes. I'll take a raincheck on that offer."

The man nodded. "Until tomorrow, then."

"How did the paperwork signing go?" Harmony asked as he put more sour cream on his baked potato.

"Fine." Jake forced himself to pay attention to her, while one corner of his brain mulled over the events at the Purple Onion. "I've never purchased a building before, so it was all new to me. The company lawyers handle that."

"Are you starting repairs tomorrow?"

She'd worn her deep blue dress again and Jake could hardly wait to give her the earrings and see them sparkle against the material. "Nope. I want you to take another walk-through first. I've got guys lined up to fix the electricity, but I hoped you'd be able to tell me if there's anything original left in the place we should preserve. Put that Victorian Era knowledge to use."

"If you wait until the weekend, I can get my landlords to help."

"I won't be here." He pulled the box out of his suit coat's pocket. It was big enough that it wouldn't be mistaken as holding a ring. "That's why I made you a copy of the key."

She scrunched her forehead. "That's not a key."

"Open it and see."

Her mouth dropped. With trembling fingers, she lifted the earrings. "These are gorgeous, Jake. You shouldn't have."

"Just a little thank you for helping me find the first house for my new venture."

"They're too expensive for me to accept."

"I got them on sale." Well, for a bargain. He'd received a major discount in exchange for a loose opal he'd 'found.' "Put them on. I've been imagining how they'll lay on your shoulders when I take you to bed tonight."

He loved watching her cheeks turn red. But she knew how to get back at him. As if in slow motion, she took out one of her tiny gold studs and laid it on the box. Then, the second one. She removed one of the dangling earrings from the cardboard holder, dipped her napkin in her water glass, and cleaned the post. She repeated the process with the other earring.

Jake took a bite of his steak and enjoyed the show.

With a wink, she picked up the first earring and

draped it across her hand. "See how it sparkles in the light?" she asked sweetly.

Two could play the game. "When I undo your bun, it'll be hard to see. Your hair will cover it."

"I guess you'd better get a good look now." She stuck the post through the little hole in her ear and slipped on the backing. "What do you think?"

"It's even more beautiful with you wearing it."

Her blush deepened. "How hard did you work on that line?"

He smirked. "One down and one to go."

She ignored him in favor of paying attention to her chicken. "What's the equivalent gift for a man?"

Jake had spent enough time with her to understand where her thoughts had gone. "Cufflinks, I suppose, although not many men wear them these days. Maybe a tie tack?"

"Look around, Jake. We're in the fanciest restaurant in Oak Grove and there are only a few men with ties." She picked up the second earring and put it in. "You're all dressed up and sexy, and you aren't wearing one. And you're the best-looking man here."

He was surprised at how much the compliment meant to him, especially coming from her. "Thank you. And the earrings do everything for you I hoped they would."

"Would you get mad if I ran away to the restroom to see them?"

The saleslady had taken care of that. "There's a mirror under the cotton pad. The house key is buried under that."

"You think of everything!" She dug the little mirror out and examined herself. "They are gorgeous. Thank you. They're the best gift I've gotten in forever."

"You'll keep them on for me tonight, right?"

She arched an eyebrow, leaned forward, and whispered, "Between you and me? I suspect your chances are looking good."

✻ ✻ ✻

He woke to the smell of coffee and Harmony singing in the shower. At least, he assumed it was singing. She was off-key and out of rhythm. He'd finally discovered something she wasn't good at.

The earrings lay on the bedside table, his shorts were on the bedroom floor, and Jake remembered taking his pants off in the front room before coming to bed the previous night. His shirt was out there, too. As much as he would have liked to take his time, he understood Harmony wasn't comfortable with him being there after she'd gone to work. He could get in anytime he wanted, but that was still his secret.

He was fully dressed and sipping on a cup of coffee when she exited the bathroom. "Anything exciting happening today?" Her idea of excitement and his were different, but he loved how she found joy in the little things.

"We've got story hour for the toddlers. And it's Thursday, so Mrs. Eckart will be in for her weekly rant about the adult books having too much sex in them. Are you coming by for lunch?"

"Probably not. I need to do another walk-through at the house and talk to a plumber, so I don't know when I'll be able to break free. But can I see you tonight?"

"How about I make supper?"

"Some of your famous spaghetti?" He'd spotted several packages of it in the freezer. "I'll stop and pick up a loaf of Italian bread to go with it."

"That sounds good. Wear a coat. They're predicting snow."

He was from the South and didn't own a coat. He also had limited experience driving in snow, which might become an issue for today's job. "Thanks for the heads up. I'll be careful."

❋ ❋ ❋

By the time his phone pinged for an incoming message, Jake had showered and shaved. The meeting place was at a local bank, and he dressed for the occasion. A simple black suit and a pale blue button-down shirt, but no tie. Basically, the same outfit he'd worn for the closing on the house, just a fresh shirt. He didn't want to outshine his employer.

He pulled in two minutes early. Punctual, but not overanxious. The instructions asked that he wait in his car, which he did, but he parked in a spot where he could keep his eye on everything. When the black BMW sedan showed up at the set time, he assumed it was his ride. It looked like it had plenty of power under the hood, and he was eager to test out what it was capable of.

When the man from the previous day climbed out

of the car, Jake understood why he wanted a driver. He clung to the door frame to raise himself upright, reached in his pocket, and took out a telescoping cane. Jake's immediate guess was that he could maneuver well enough around town but couldn't handle long distances.

The man waved, and Jake went to meet him.

"Good morning," the man said. "You're right on time. I like that. Wait here, I have business in the bank before we get started."

"That's fine, but one question. Are we going to exchange names, or do you want me to call you sir?" Jake suspected the man knew his name, but he wanted the rules to be clear.

The man grinned. "Carl said you were sharp. For appearances, you can refer to me as Mr. Carmillo, but between you and me, it's Rick. Rikhard, but I go by Rick. And you're Jake, but I didn't catch your last name."

*Because Carl didn't know my last name.* "Hennessey. Pleased to meet you, Rick."

"The keys are in the car, if you want to check it out. This should only take a few minutes."

Jake familiarized himself with the controls while Rick took care of business. Headlights, turn signals, windshield wipers, shifting. He was disappointed it was an automatic, but that was okay for one day. He wondered when the bodyguard part of the job would kick in.

When Rick came out, Jake hopped out of the car and around to the passenger side. "Front or back?"

"Front. I can scoot the seat back and have more room to stretch out. But that doesn't mean I want to spend the trip talking."

"Fair enough." Jake was used to long, quiet drives, so the setup didn't bother him. He held the door open while Rick got settled in the seat and fastened his seatbelt.

Jake wasn't sure if Rick was reading his phone or sleeping, but when the signs indicated Erie was ten miles ahead, he cleared his throat. "We're almost there. I need directions to your destination."

Rick's head jerked up. "Already? That was a smooth trip. You'll stay on 79 until you get to exit 180. From there it's a right-hand turn."

At first, Jake thought they were going to the mall, but Rick directed him to a back street, past a strip mall, then to a house. Clearly it wasn't an ordinary house. It had bars on the windows, a security camera in plain view, and a guard dog behind a tall wire fence. Jake suspected the front door was reinforced, too.

He parked and waited for his instructions.

"Here's where you earn your money," Rick said. "From here on out, I'm Mr. Carmillo. You'll walk with me to the front door and inside. Once you are sure it's safe, come back to the car and keep your eye on the neighborhood. Then you'll do it again in reverse when I complete my business. Shouldn't take more than fifteen or twenty minutes."

"And if I spot trouble?"

"Use your judgment. Take care of it if you can, but if you need to call the cops, go for it. The business's security feed will alert us to any problems, and I'll know to stay put."

The plan sounded solid. "It's not the first time you've done this, Mr. Carmillo."

"No, and I haven't had an issue yet. Let's get this show on the road."


Everything went as planned, except Rick stayed inside longer than fifteen minutes—it was closer to twenty-five—when the door cracked open. But in that time, nothing had happened except for a few cars driving by and a cat strolling down the sidewalk, which upset the dog.

Jake walked Rick back to the car, and soon they were on their way.

Rick sighed and reclined his seat. "That's a weight off my shoulders."

"I'm glad to hear it, Mr. Carmillo." Although curiosity crawled up his spine, Jake didn't ask any questions.

"It's back to Rick unless we need to make a stop. Can you find your way to Oak Grove from here?"

"Sure enough."

Jake anticipated a smooth ride home, doing his best to impress Rick, although he might have been sleeping again. He'd had his bad luck on this road; there'd be no way he'd be involved in another major accident.

But the car three places back bothered him. Too many cars flashed by, and that one was always there. He slowed and set the cruise control to the speed limit. Any normal driver would soon pass them.

Rick looked up from his phone. "Is there a problem?"

"Not sure. Either we've got an unmarked state trooper on our tail, or we have trouble. Do you have anything in the vehicle that the police would object to?"

"No. What's the plan?"

"I'm doing precisely the posted speed and staying in the middle of the lane. I can do this all day. If that's the police, they'll run a tag check, see the car is legal, and give up their quest to pull me over."

"And if it isn't the police?"

"Then it'll come down to the better car and the better driver. And our odds are pretty damn good."

# Chapter 17

Jake checked the rearview mirror. The suspect car was still there, three positions back. "Normally I wouldn't ask this," he said. "But what are you carrying? It's not drugs or guns." And it wasn't precious stones, because Jake would have known that instinctively.

Rick fidgeted in the passenger seat. "You can't tell anyone."

"That's a given." Jake considered taking the exit a mile ahead, but he didn't know whether it led to another major highway or a country road, so it was a bad bet.

"Stamps. I collect stamps. And the one I bought today I've wanted for over twenty years."

All Jake knew about stamps was that most of them were worth face value while others were worth thousands. He'd never attempted to enter that market.

Rick stared straight ahead. "This stamp cost a quarter of a million dollars."

Jake shot Rick a sideways glance but kept his composure. No wonder Rick wanted a bodyguard. "And you want to get to the bank before it closes so you can put it in your safe deposit box."

"I have a safe at home. I want to spend one night admiring it and take it to the bank tomorrow. It'd be a shame to own it and never enjoy being able to hold it."

Jake understood, but that wasn't information he could share. Besides, the other car had switched lanes. "Brace yourself," he said. "Keep your eyes front and center. Don't give them any excuse to stop us."

He tapped the brake to take the car out of cruise control, then let his foot hover above the gas pedal.

"You've done this before." Rick reached for the dashboard.

"Misspent youth."

The dark gray vehicle was traveling in his blind spot. That didn't stop Jake from knowing it was there. "How did you get into stamp collecting?" he asked to ease the tension.

"My mother gave me a beginner's collecting kit for my tenth birthday. Which I hated. But the stamps were space related, which I loved. I ended up asking for more stamps for Christmas, and here we are. I still have those original ones. They're worth only a few dollars, but are priceless to me."

*Like Harmony and her copy of the Three Musketeers.*

The gray car pulled alongside. If anything was going to happen, this would be the time. Jake adjusted his grip on the steering wheel.

The car sped up and moved past them, and Jake verified the occupants wore uniforms. That, and the markings on the side, confirmed his first guess. "Yep, state troopers. But I can't figure out why they were so persistent. Normally, a follow only lasts a few miles. Unless this car matches the description of a different one and they had to wait for the plates to be run."

Or they'd ID'd him and were checking if he'd stolen the vehicle. The state guys could be working with anyone from the Feds to some local agency. He swallowed hard and wished for a drink to ease his sudden headache.

Rick let go of the dash. "The only time I take this out of town is for my trips to buy or sell stamps."

"It's a pleasure to drive. I had fun."

They made it back to Oak Grove on schedule, even though Jake stuck to the speed limit the rest of the way. Back at the bank, Jake held the driver's side door open while Rick maneuvered into the seat. He moved slower, the ride apparently having worn him out. Before closing the door, Rick unlocked the glove box, retrieved an envelope, and gave it to Jake.

"That's for you," Rick said. "I appreciate you stepping in at the last minute."

Jake wouldn't open the envelope until later. That would be against the rules. "Do you want me to follow you home?"

"It's close enough to my normal working hours that no one will think twice about it." Rick smiled. "Besides, nothing ever happens in Oak Grove."

That wasn't true, but Jake nodded in agreement. He tapped the roof of Rick's car, shut the door, and stepped back.

As he walked back to the Charger, he calculated if he would have time to change clothes and make a quick trip to the old house. The ideas on a home remodeling show had inspired him. It would be fun to incorporate them into the few bits of information that Harmony had dredged up about the house's history.

"How was your day?" Harmony asked as he placed the loaf of store-bought Italian on the plate she'd put out.

"Not bad." It had gotten considerably better when he'd opened the envelope and found a thousand dollars in crisp bills. "But I can't decide on a color scheme for the first floor. Did you come across any information on the original paint?"

"Nothing. I'm hoping if I scratch deep enough on a wall, I can find a trace of it. But there's no guarantee we can recreate it." She took the butter out of the fridge and set it on the table.

He grabbed her from behind and nuzzled her neck. "Smells terrific."

"The spaghetti?"

"You." He kissed her ear and let her go. "The spaghetti too, but mostly you."

She inhaled. "Did you change your aftershave?"

*Shit*. He'd dropped by the Purple Onion and had been invited out back to partake in some high-quality weed. "Like cleanser? I scrubbed the bathroom sink at the house with cleaning wipes." He raised each arm and sniffed his armpits. "I promise I took a shower this morning."

"Eager to get the utilities turned on?"

She'd bought it. He almost felt guilty. "Not until they replace the kitchen wiring. I don't trust running even one appliance in there. And none of the outlets are three-pronged."

She planted a peck on his cheek. "Worry about it later. Supper's ready."

Jake wondered whose life he'd hijacked. Because this one didn't belong to him.

❋ ❋ ❋

"Jade attracts good luck." The red-headed raised one necklace in the air. "And this red agate is for passion." She was pushing a selection of jewelry and essential oils. Jake was one of four men in the audience, and the other three looked as if they'd been dragged there by their wives. Other vendors in the hotel conference room in downtown Seattle displayed everything from plastic storage bowls to fake flowers.

Most of what this vendor was selling was dyed quartzite and not true jade. Except for that one piece, a necklace of authentic stones. She didn't seem to know the difference. All she knew about her wares was what the brochures the company provided told her, testimony to the lack of training the company provided.

His sources claimed she kept her jewelry in a safe deposit box when she wasn't at a show, even the cheap stuff. A few days of surveillance had confirmed the information, and he'd changed his normal tactics.

He sat through the entire sales pitch, then hung

back from the group sniffing the various scented oils. The trick was to not appear too eager but to make his request when the saleslady was overwhelmed and too busy to pay attention to him.

He picked up a pair of coral earrings, pretended to study them, and put them back in their spot. Moving on to a cheaply made crystal ring, he held it up to the light, and then returned it to its place.

"Can I help you?" the saleslady asked.

"I'm looking for a gift for my girlfriend. She usually wears silver jewelry, and I want to surprise her with something different."

"What message do you want to send?"

He'd listened to her nonsense and knew how to answer. "She's been through some rough times. Lost her job, although she's working again. One guy she works with is a creep, and I need to protect her. What kind of stone should I give her?"

"For protection? Jade is perfect. Look at these and I'll be right back." She went over to ring up a customer buying a variety of the oils.

Jake picked up several fake jade necklaces, held them up to the light, then returned them to the display in a different order. He quirked his mouth and picked up the true jade necklace again. Turning his back to the counter, he raised his hand to study it in a vague trace of sunlight. That was all the time he needed to swap it with a cheap necklace he'd bought at another store. The high-quality necklace ended up in his pocket and the fake one on the display.

"Have you decided?" the saleslady asked.

He fingered a pair of cheap fake-jade earrings. "I like these, but do you offer any discounts?"

The essential oil he'd bought as part of the package deal hit the garbage can on his way out of the hotel that hosted the convention. A little girl playing by the fountain outside got the earrings. The real jade necklace was headed overseas, and that was as much as Jake had been told. It was someone else's problem to get it there.

❊ ❊ ❊

He'd fallen into a pattern. Routines were a trap, but he couldn't talk himself out of this one. On the weekends, he picked up whatever shifts he could as a bouncer. Every other week, he checked on the house and made time to be with Harmony. In between, he chased that elusive rainbow of finding another big score.

His sources had dried up. He'd been to a society wedding but didn't come away with any prize beyond a simple sterling-silver charm bracelet. Desperation had led him to this traveling jewelry exhibit at the Art Museum in Chicago.

There'd be no chance of walking away with anything more than a speck of dust, but he wandered through the displays, admiring the quality and variety of jewelry. One piece in particular caught his eye, and he imagined it gracing Harmony's neck.

The necklace, a ruby and diamond bib-style set in white gold, was in its own case, with several additional layers of security. He didn't have the skill to break through the system. It would take an inside job to steal it.

With his hands clasped behind his back to avoid the temptation of touching the case, he read the information placard. The piece was of British heritage, dating to the 1600s. The family that had owned it sold it after World War II. A long list of celebrities had bought or borrowed the necklace before it was put on display in the jewelry museum twenty years earlier.

Aware of the pair of middle-aged women crowding in, he moved along to admire another exhibit. It was a pink diamond, the current trend in rings, but Jake preferred classic stones. Moving to another room didn't end the uncomfortable instinct that he was being watched. Not by someone in the area, but by an overhead camera.

If law enforcement had identified him, that didn't bode well for his career. He couldn't live off the petty thefts that people assumed were accidents and turned into their insurance companies without filing a police claim. And the more money he sunk into the old house, the more he realized it would never turn a profit.

To throw off his tail, he spent time he hadn't planned on exploring other exhibits in the museum. On the way out, he couldn't resist buying a postcard featuring the necklace, as well as a cheap replica. A friend of a friend could use them to create a fake that would look as good as the actual necklace to an untrained eye.

The whiskey was poured before Jake got to the bar

at the Purple Onion. Danny, the daytime bartender, inclined his head towards the office. Nobody had to say a word. Jake understood the message.

He stopped to say hello to several of the regulars. Sam mimed smoking a joint, but Jake shook his head. Business first.

He half-expected to find Rick in the office with Carl, but guessed wrong. Carl was alone. "I've only been in town an hour and everyone knows I'm here already?" Jake asked as he sat.

Carl grinned. "You stay at the same motel every time."

A habit Jake needed to break. He wondered which of the motel's employees was Carl's spy.

"I could toss a mattress on the floor up at the old house." Jake grimaced. "But I enjoy having electricity and running water."

"You should hire someone to keep an eye on it. People passing through town have tried to take advantage of the space."

In other words, someone in Carl's web of friends had chased them off. "The place is already a money pit. I'll have to see how I can stretch the budget. How can I repay the favor?"

Carl placed a shot glass in front of Jake and filled it with the good stuff, not the rotgut they served out front. "We've got a situation. A friend got thrown out of his house by his wife."

Jake expected what came next. He took a swig of the whiskey and swished it in his mouth before swallowing. It smelled like a trap. Or an initiation to the inner workings of Carl's circle of friends.

"Her new boyfriend moved in and changed the locks. My friend needs to get in and get his stuff. Rumor has it you can help."

Jake downed what remained of the whiskey. "Despite the rumors, I won't do anything illegal."

Carl grunted and refilled the glass. "The lease is in my friend's name. He has every right to be there. But the cops won't interfere in a domestic situation. Told him to take it to court. Which he doesn't have the money for."

"Leaving your friend stranded."

Carl nodded. "What complicates things is that the boyfriend is the brother of one of the town's cops."

"He'd be a fool to try to get in when his wife was there." Jake swirled the whiskey as he thought. "I hate to pass up an opportunity to stick it to the police. When do both the wife and the boyfriend leave? Nighttime preferably. Is there a dog?"

The corners of Carl's mouth twitched. "Anything else you need?"

"The address. And a car I can borrow to scope out the neighborhood ahead of time. Mine is too recognizable. I won't go inside. Or stick around. Once the door is unlocked, I'm gone."

"I can set that up. What day works for you??"

"Wednesday nights are my friend's nights to spend with her girlfriends. She's been skipping them or taking me along when I'm in town." It had the added benefit of being the night when the cops had the fewest staff on duty. "I can beg off, and that'll give me the entire night to help without her suspecting anything. Let's hope it fits into the wife's schedule."

"You sound like an old married man sneaking out to have a drink with his friends."

Jake guzzled the last of his whiskey and stared at the empty glass. "That'll never happen. She's too good for me."

# Chapter 18

Jake had asked Harmony to wear her finest dress. He wore his second-best suit, because he didn't want to outshine her, and no restaurant in Oak Grove met the standards for his 'high society' clothes. He even stopped and picked up a bouquet to present to her when he knocked on her door, wanting the night to be perfect, one she'd remember forever.

When she opened the door, air rushed from his lungs. The silky red dress clung to her in all the right spots, and the neckline was cut deep enough to not leave everything to his imagination. The replica necklace tucked in his pocket appeared to be made to match the dress. He'd ended up paying far more for the necklace than expected, but once it was draped over Harmony's bust, it would be worth every penny.

He found his breath and his voice. "For you," he said, extending the bouquet. "The most beautiful woman I've ever known."

The scarlet in her cheeks wasn't quite as red as her dress. "Check you out," she said. "Every woman in town will be jealous of me."

"I could stand here and admire you all night," Jake said. "But we have reservations at The Grove. I'm looking forward to showing you off."


He'd planned on giving her the necklace after supper but couldn't wait. Halfway to the restaurant, he pulled over. With raised eyebrows, she asked, "What's wrong?"

"You're missing something." He pulled the black velvet bag holding the jewelry from his pocket. "Will you wear this tonight? Please?"

She emptied the bag into her lap and held up the necklace. The stones shimmered in the headlights of a car headed the other direction. Her mouth widened. "Jake, it's lovely. But I can't..."

"Don't say anything but thank you. And then put it on."

"It goes so well with my dress..."

She wasn't convinced yet. "Please?" He batted his eyes.

Harmony succumbed to the temptation and raised it to her chest. "How does it look?" she asked.

"Better than I imagined. Do you need help to fasten it?"

"Sure." She twisted, and he stroked her neck before securing the clasp. Later, he'd kiss that one spot just below her left ear that made her go crazy.


The atmosphere was cozy and private, the food

perfect, the service attentive and the company all Jake could desire.

"It's like Halloween for grownups," Harmony giggled as she took a bite of her 'medium-medium' steak.

He preferred his steak done medium-rare. "What do you mean?" he asked.

She dipped her head toward the left. "Don't look now, but that couple over there? They are the Russells. When they come to the library, they normally dress in old sweatpants."

Jake couldn't help himself and peeked. Mr. Russell's outfit was a too-big black suit, while Mrs. Russell wore a dark blue dress with shoulder pads, most likely something she'd bought years ago. Her silver-tone necklace was costume jewelry. Good quality, but not valuable. "I see what you mean."

She tilted her head to the right. "And the lady over there? That's Mrs. Thames. She's a nurse at the hospital, and she's always in her scrubs. She's really pretty all dressed up."

*How would Harmony react if she found out my entire life was spent playing dress-up and switching personalities?* Jake reached across the table and covered her hand with his. "I don't even have to see to know she isn't as beautiful as you."

"You say that like it's true." She rolled her eyes. "Come Christmas time, people will dress even fancier. Management goes all out for decorations and people go overboard to impress." She sighed. "The city puts up the same decorations every year. They claim it's tradition but, the truth is, they don't have money to buy new ones."

He hadn't celebrated Christmas for years. And he wouldn't steal from holiday parties, because he didn't want to ruin someone else's joy. Where could he get the money to buy her a present to rival the necklace? Which looked amazing against her skin. He lost track of the conversation as the fake diamonds sparkled in the dim light. He almost believed they were real.

Jake rubbed the itch at the back of his neck. Something was off, and he couldn't identify what. He wasn't doing anything illegal, and he'd refrained from even the smallest of jewelry heists in town. They'd even turned in the necklace with a single pearl that he and Harmony found in the park to the police.

So, he ignored the warning and tried to enjoy his time with her. Once he ran out of money and only had his income as a bouncer, she'd drop him and he'd fade away into loneliness. She needed to find an honest man to share her life with.

They held hands as they walked back to the Charger. "That was amazing," she said. "Thank you."

"We'll have to do it again," he answered. "It was nice, getting dressed up."

"It was, wasn't it? But I got tired of people staring at us. At least, I guess that's what made me antsy."

She'd felt it, too? That wasn't a good sign. He played it off. "It's your fault for being so darn beautiful, Angel."

"It'll be a shame to take these clothes off."

"I am very much looking forward to taking that dress off you," Jake said, his voice husky. "But we'll leave the necklace on."

She brushed his cheek with the tips of her fingers and winked as he held open the door for her to get in the car. "We'll see." But the sparkle in her eye held promise.

The slow dance to Harmony's bedroom started at the front door with a gentle kiss as Jake helped her take off her coat. Once the coat was hung on its hanger, he took off his suitcoat, loosened his tie, and unbuttoned the top two buttons of his shirt. Her eyes glittered as bright as the fake diamonds that hung around her neck, and he wanted to rip the dress from her shoulders and get the show on the road.

She took his coat from his arm, laid it on the back of her couch, and patted the seat.

He knew the drill. She wanted to cuddle. And kiss. And see where it went from there.

"Do you want something to drink?" she asked.

He'd limited himself to one at supper, worried that the cops were targeting him. He'd seen three police vehicles on the short drive to the restaurant and another on the way back. "You have any beer?"

It was an hour before they made it to her bedroom. Once he'd helped Harmony out of her dress, when she pretended that she couldn't get it unzipped, he lost track of time. At least he convinced her to leave the necklace on. He was only partly aware of her taking it off in the middle of the night.

He woke when her alarm went off but Jake stayed in bed so she could have the bathroom to herself. When she finished and headed to the kitchen, he crawled out, pulled on his shorts and dress pants, then traced her steps. She sat at the kitchen table, drinking her coffee and reading the paper.

"Too chilly to sit on the steps?" he asked as he sipped from the cup she had waiting for him.

"It's almost winter. It's cold outside."

"I'm from the South. To me, it was freezing two months ago."

"Wimp." She hid her grin behind her cup.

"Now, remember, I'm working tonight. You're on your own for your Girls' Night Out thing."

She fluttered her eyelashes. "I'll miss you."

He tapped her nose. "I want you to have fun."

She reached into the pocket of her robe and pulled out the necklace. "And I want you to take this back. It's way too expensive for me to take as a gift. Return it and use the money on the house or something." She shook her head. "Let's not argue and ruin what was a perfect night."

He couldn't break the illusion and reveal the necklace was a fake. And he didn't know everything about women's clothing, but her dress had been expensive. It hadn't come from a local pawnshop or department store. Had Carl been right after all when he claimed she had money?

It didn't make sense. Jake stuck the necklace into his pants pocket. He'd dig deeper into the riddle that was Harmony Duprie later.

❋ ❋ ❋

At a quarter to eleven that night, Jake answered the knock on his motel door. The front desk clerk handed him an envelope. "Message for you," the young man said. "I'm supposed to wait for an answer."

Jake ripped the envelope open. "Blue car in the parking lot," the note read. "Cops. Leave the back way."

He didn't check for the car. "What back way?"

"The break between the building with the soda machine? There's a staff-only door. It's unlocked. Follow the hall and it'll take you to the back office. Your ride will pick you up there."

Jake took a ten out of his wallet and handed it to the clerk. "How do you know Carl?"

"He's my uncle." The man grinned and stuck the money in his pocket. "See you in a few."

Jake tugged on the door as he left to double-check that he'd locked it. Not that it would stop a determined cop from smashing the door in. With all the confidence of James Bond, he strolled towards the soda machine in black jeans and a light t-shirt with a black one underneath. He wished he could have added a jacket to his outfit, but he didn't want to look like he was going somewhere. His tools were in his jeans pocket.

The clerk was talking to another customer out front, so, in the darkened back office, Jake stood and waited. His neck itched, a sure sign he was being observed, but he trusted Carl as much as he trusted anyone. Except for Harmony. She was on a different level.

It didn't take long for the clerk to enter the office and eyeball Jake. "Your ride should be here in about five minutes. Do you need a coat? It's below freezing."

"I didn't want the cop to think I was leaving," Jake explained.

"No problem. People leave crap behind all the time. I think we've got something that'll work." He dug through a cardboard box in the corner and pulled out a black jacket. "Try this." He tossed it to Jake.

It wasn't a perfect fit, but it was better than nothing.

The back door opened. Jake recognized the man from the bar, although he'd never talked to him. "Cops still out front?" the man asked.

The clerk nodded. "They haven't even gone for coffee."

"I wonder who the snitch is. We'll handle that later." He turned to Jake. "You can call me Bill. That's not my name, but I'll answer to it."

Bill thought this was a game. For Jake, it was never a game.


Daytime surveillance had provided Jake with a sense of the neighborhood. Small older homes, not falling apart, but most needed tender loving care. The kind of houses filled with elderly people whose kids had grown up, left home, and left town. Where the lawns still got mowed every Saturday, even if spots got missed and the clippings didn't get raked. Where in the old days, nobody locked their houses when they were home. Those days were gone, partly because of people like him.

Or the houses were rented out. He hadn't spotted evidence of young kids. It made his job easier. Parents wouldn't be up in the middle of the night, tending to a crying baby, and glimpse him in action. With no college in town, Jake didn't have to worry about college kids partying in the middle of the night and attracting cops.

Two blocks from the target, Bill leaned forward and peered out the window at the cars along the darkened street. Most of the streetlights were out. "Can you believe it?" Bill asked. "Just our luck. A kid with a BB gun shot out the lights last night and the city hasn't got them replaced yet."

He flashed his car's headlights at an old pickup parked along the street. The flame from a cigarette lighter flared and disappeared. The players had taken their positions.

The wife and her boyfriend were at karaoke night at the cowboy bar. The dumped husband would never see Jake's face. By the time he got to his house, the back door would be unlocked and Jake no more than a wisp of a shadow. As simple as the job was, Jake's nerves were strung as tight as guitar strings. He didn't work well with others. Or on their terms, not his.

Bill drove past the house, turned the corner to the cross street, and parked. "You sure you don't want me to wait here for you?"

"No." Jake shook his head as he opened his door. "If something goes wrong, I don't want you caught up in it."

"Got it. I'll wait for you over by the school then."

The school was four blocks away. A long stroll in the frosty night air, but it would give Jake time to come down from the adrenalin rush he got after a job. This one was different because there'd be no reward at the end. Still, he needed to treat it as if the Queen's crown waited for him. He stood, took a deep breath, and closed the car door without answering.

He waited until Bill drove away to start the journey to the back door of the house in the middle of the block. Under the cover of a hedge separating two yards, he headed towards the alley. Broken wooden fences hid him from the houses on either side. Despite the frigid air, he broke into a sweat, and stopped in a shadow to check his surroundings. His gut screamed at him to abandon the mission despite there being no sign of trouble. But he hated to disappoint Carl.

The plastic gloves he'd taken from the housekeeper's cart were too big when he pulled them on. He'd expected that. After easing past the garbage cans and through the open gate, Jake stopped in the darkness created by an old tree in the backyard to make another assessment of the situation. A dog barked nearby, and he waited until the murmur of a voice and the sound of a door closing told him the pooch was inside his owner's house.

In a low crouch, he dashed across the yard. The bare bulb that illuminated the entrance was on, and Jake slid off the glove on his right hand to unscrew it, burning his fingers. A small price to pay for the resulting darkness.

The lock itself, a standard big-box store purchase, didn't present a challenge. Jake inserted his most-loved pick, closed his eyes, twisted the tool, and 'felt' the pins drop into place. He twisted the knob, but only opened the door a crack before closing it again. His work was complete. If anyone had been watching, all they would have seen was him trying the door handle and then leaving.

The walk to the school should have been relaxing, but the feeling that someone was following didn't go away. He stopped long enough at a trash can to throw away the plastic gloves. Adrenalin pumped through his veins, and he twitched at every sound and each wavering shadow. When he finally got to safety, he'd crash and crash hard.

Bill's beat-up car was a welcome sight. Jake tapped on the back window to wake Bill up before opening the passenger-side door.

"How'd it go?" Bill asked as he started the engine.

Rookie mistake. Bill should have left the engine running, and the defroster turned on. The front window was fogged up, evidence that the car was occupied. But Jake wouldn't say anything about it.

"Tell Carl to tell his friend to make it a quick in-and-out. Something doesn't smell right."

"Cops?"

"I can't put my finger on it." Jake took his tools out of his pocket and stuffed them under the seat. That way, the tools wouldn't be on him if they were stopped and frisked.

While Bill called Carl, Jake closed his eyes and concentrated on his breathing, trying to get his heartbeat down. What was it about this job that bothered him? Was it because he was breaking his rule about not sullying the waters where he lived? Where Harmony lived, that's where he wanted to be.

Even lost in his thoughts, he was aware when Bill pulled onto the street. And that they took the long route to get back to the hotel. When they stopped two blocks away, he wondered if Bill had read his mind. Or learned something.

He retrieved his tool kit before climbing out of the car. "Don't expect to see me for a while."

"Leaving town?" Bill asked.

Jake shook his head. "That would be suspicious. No, I'll be working on the house. Right where the cops expect to find me."

# Chapter 19

Despite the air conditioning in the Houston mansion, the back of Jake's shirt clung to him. The gold filigree necklace and earring set seemed so close, yet so far away. He'd been rummaging in the master bedroom's closet when the Walters returned home early. He had made it to their spare bedroom without being caught, and now he was stuck. So far, they hadn't noticed anything out of place. If one of them took the garbage out, they'd realize the back door was unlocked.

The three pieces had a buyer in Brazil, and if Jake stole the collection, he'd be set for several months. But it was looking as if a jail cell awaited him. While he strained to hear the conversation between the couple, his mind worked on a cover story. The cops would never buy the line about the security system being disabled and Jake, after seeing another man run from the house, coming in to check and make sure everyone was okay before calling law enforcement.

"Honey, will you get my jacket out of the closet in the little bedroom?" the wife asked from the hallway. "It's getting chilly. And don't forget your phone this time."

With the merest whisper of movement, Jake scrambled to the far side of the bed. He was too big to crawl under it, but laying on the floor behind it should hide him. The light in the room turned on, and Jake held his breath as the closet door slid open. "Star gazing," Mr. Walter grumbled. "We haven't done that since we dated. Like you'll be able to see the stars for all the city lights." Then, loudly, "Which coat, Darling?"

"Never mind," came the answer. "I'm going to wear my sweater instead. Grab one for yourself."

"I'm not as cold-blooded as you are," Mr. Walter mumbled. "But if I don't take a jacket, you'll fuss."

Hangers screeched against the rod, followed by the rustle of fabric and the door sliding closed. The room darkened. Still, Jake didn't move except to release a silent breath, then fill his lungs.

He waited until a door closed. And waited longer for the engine of their oversized truck to rumble to life. He stayed on the floor until silence told him they'd driven away. Had they reset the alarm? How was he going to leave the house without it blaring? But if he remembered the setup, the system had an override button on the interior panels that allowed for a five-minute pause. He'd get out, close the door behind him, and the Walters would never know.

Using his elbows and knees, he crawled across the floor to the doorway, and rechecked his surroundings. The lights were off, except for the small nightlights plugged into almost every outlet. Which of the Walters feared the dark?

As long as Mrs. Walter hadn't moved the collection in the past few minutes, he'd be out of the house in no time. The curtains in the master remained closed, and now on his feet, he worked by the shadowy illumination the nightlights provided. By touch alone, Jake worked the dial, listening to one pin at a time drop into place until the door on the safe swung open, revealing the jewelry box containing his prize.

He slipped the necklace and earrings into the velvet bag from his pocket, exchanging the pieces for the small rocks he'd brought. They weighed the same as the jewelry, and until Mrs. Walters opened the box, she'd never realize the switch had been made. Jake felt no guilt, because the pieces had been confiscated from a Jewish family during World War II and were being returned to a descendant. At least, that was the story. Jake didn't care if it was true.

What he cared about was getting back to the borrowed vehicle half a mile away. In a more elaborate setup than normal, his Charger sat at a mechanic's shop in Atlanta, 'getting the brakes worked on.' Then, he'd driven to Houston in a car from a small auto sales place. In Houston, he'd parked that auto at a fleabag motel and then rented a car from the pay-as-you-go dealership next door. Cash transactions, of course.

He clung to the edge of the stairs and reached the first floor without a creak. Crouching low, he crept through the dining room and into the kitchen. Almost there.

The deep rumble of an oversized truck halted his progress. He dropped to the floor with his back against the island and groaned. Why had the Walters returned so soon?

But he could use their arrival to his advantage. The moment they opened the front door, he'd dash out the back. If the alarm sounded, they'd blame it on hitting the wrong key and try again. A moment was all it would take to make his getaway.

On his hands and knees, he crawled towards the back door, trying to figure out the timing. Only a few seconds separated success from failure. If the Walters came in through the rear entrance, he was doomed. In a crouch, he waited and listened for the opening of the front door, while monitoring the LED lights on the security panel by the back door.

"I can't believe you forgot your phone."

Mrs. Walter's voice carried through the house, and the lights on the panel flickered off. Jake rose, turned the handle, opened the door, and slid into the night air.

Three long blocks later, he stopped to listen for sirens and determine his next step. In the shadow of a thick hedge, he peeled off his black T-shirt, revealing a pale blue one underneath it. He shoved the black one into the middle of the foliage, where it wouldn't be spotted until the gardener trimmed the bushes.

The circuitous route to the car took twice as long as the direct one but assured him that no alarm had been raised. Only the occasional vehicle driving by or the faint cheers from a distant high school football game disturbed the night silence.

Back at the motel, even the half bottle of whiskey didn't help him sleep. Had he lost his edge?

Before leaving town, he stopped by the post office to mail a postcard from Albuquerque, and a box for his niece. It contained an assortment of brightly colored toys and fake jewelry he'd picked up from a thrift store. Junk. No one would suspect it held a treasure.

The round-about route Jake picked for the trip home took him through Dallas, Little Rock, and Memphis. He stopped in each to fill the gas tank and buy a postcard. By the time he got back, a thick envelope waited for him in his post office box. Newspaper clippings and cash, the first payment of three for the Houston collection. It was enough to cover his bills with some left over to sink into the house and to send Harmony flowers, an apology for his absence.

He needed to get out of Atlanta. The shadows that followed him when he was at Shaggy's were getting sloppy and easy to spot. That, and his room had been searched. There had been nothing obvious, just small things out of place. His aftershave moved to far towards the front of the sink. The TV set to a local news station instead of the movie channel. His landlord denied it, of course, but he seemed to be smoking a more potent class of weed than usual when Jake sought him out. Or was that because Jake had paid up his rent several months in advance?

Oak Grove was the obvious place to hang out for

a few weeks. He'd work on the house during the day and spend his nights making love to Harmony. Or go to Chicago and hide out at Ruby's while he determined his next step. He shook his head. No. Sharing Ruby's bed wasn't an option.

He left his car in the lot at a hotel near the airport, paid for long-term parking, then took a bus to one of Atlanta's suburbs. There, he visited a pay-here car dealer, and slipped the sales agent a nice wad of cash to let him 'try out' a vehicle for a few days. He took a meandering route north, sticking mostly to two-lane highways and small towns, avoiding the temptation of visiting anyplace where there might be jewelry worth stealing. Each day, he stopped at a real-estate firm and checked their listings for old houses to maintain his cover story. Each night for three nights, he found an empty store lot to catch a few hours sleep. He hoped to use the trip to flush out any followers, but the tingle at the back of his neck must have been paranoia because the normal tricks didn't work. Unexpected turns, backtracking, sitting in busy parking lots and watching the traffic flow all proved unsuccessful.

On the northern outskirts of Pittsburgh, three cop cars, with lights flashing and sirens blaring, hurtled past him on the interstate and made his decision for him. At the Oak Grove exit, he pushed the gas pedal, gripped the steering wheel and heading north. Harmony didn't know he was coming, so she wouldn't be disappointed. He'd go mingle with the tourists at Niagara Falls, four hours away, and look for easy pickings to ease the itch.

It was a mistake. Too many people, too many cameras. He never knew when one might be aimed his direction. He couldn't even pick a pocket without worrying someone was capturing the moment. Jake didn't like making mistakes, especially ones putting him at risk and costing him money.

Despite the damp benches, he sat at a picnic table, pretending to stare at his phone but actually studying the crowd, looking for anyone who didn't fit. The huddle of Amish tourists was surprising but an unlikely choice. The mix of people from all over the world made picking out a culprit nearly impossible. Everybody belonged and nobody belonged.

But the place had a certain charm. The mist rising above the water, the constant roar of the falls, the hundreds of excited voices squealing at their first sight of the river tumbling over the edges of the cliffs. He wondered if Harmony had ever been here. He'd like to take her to a few of his favorite places and watch her face as she reacted to the sights. But that would never happen.

He hung out for two days, hoping to convince his unseen shadow that he was a tourist like any other. He bought postcards, ate at the tourist spots, and took the boat to the base of the Falls. To his relief, he never spotted even one piece of jewelry worth stealing, until the moment when he was relaxing in his borrowed car, watching people come and go, waiting for a sign it was time to leave.

The harried mother of three little ones sat on a bench, trying to feed the baby and keep the other two under control. The father had wandered off to a nearby gift shop. She was having a hard time taking care of them by herself.

The oldest one—Jake guessed she was five—chased after a loose ball a wind gust sent into the parking lot while the mother wasn't looking. No one else was watching either, including the driver of the car backing out of a nearby spot. Sensing a disaster in the making, Jake slammed his fist on his horn, threw open his door, and flew out of his seat.

He'd heard stories of strangers being attacked when they grabbed a kid, even when they were trying to save them, so he employed a different tactic. As the sedan backed up, he pounded first on the rear window, then on the trunk to get the driver's attention. He planted himself behind the car where the driver couldn't miss seeing him in the rearview mirror.

The car stopped, and the window rolled down. "Move, asshole," the driver, a middle-aged man, shouted, waving his left hand in the air.

Jake drooled over the Rolex on the man's wrist. The diamonds on the face sparkled in a stray beam of sunlight. Even with the old-fashioned buckle and leather strap, it was worth a small fortune. But there was no way to get it in his clutches. "There's a little kid behind the car. Did you check?"

"Then get your rugrat out of the way."

"Not mine. I'm just a concerned bystander." Jake had been careful in his liaisons. There shouldn't be any little Jakes out there anywhere.

The mother came running and grabbed the little

girl by the hand, dragging her to the sidewalk, making the ball fall. The little girl cried as it rolled away.

Jake chased after it and threw it into the small patch of grass near the picnic tables. The little girl giggled, pulled away from her mother, and ran after it. Mom shifted the baby on her hip and followed, with the middle child trailing along.

"Do I have your permission to leave now?" the man in the car grouched.

No 'thank you,' but Jake hadn't expected one. "No one's stopping you."

"Idiot," the man muttered as he shifted into reverse.

Jake stepped onto the sidewalk and tried to figure out the puzzle of the car and the watch. They didn't match. The car was an economy model, at least ten years old, and the motor had a miss. If the man could afford a Rolex, wouldn't he be able to buy a better vehicle? From the glimpse Jake got of the watch, it wasn't a counterfeit.

The man gunned his engine, drawing Jake's attention, and stuck his arm out the window, with one finger raised. It might have been wishful thinking, but Jake imagined something sparkly fell to the ground. Either that, or the man had added to his rudeness by littering. Jake didn't fight the urge, but took his sweet time strolling to the spot, heading for his hoped-for prize, acting as if he was admiring the view.

# Chapter 20

Calib Booker was his least favorite pawnbroker. Jake didn't trust him, but he'd have to do, because he had the connections needed to sell the watch. The negotiations started by giving him a bargain on gold ring. Jake had picked up the piece at a second-hand store, where he'd convinced the clerk it was gold-plated. Once Calib was in a good mood, the real prize was placed on the counter.

"The band broke, and the owner didn't even notice." Jake pointed out the worn edges on the leather strap. "I pretended to report the find to security, but instead told them I was concerned about drivers not paying attention. Complained they needed more signs warning people to be careful."

The pawnbroker, a nearly-bald man with a potbelly, stroked the Rolex, the finest item in sight. The rest of the store was as worn-down and hopeless as its customers. "What name did you give them?"

The ID had been fake, and the phone number belonged to a restaurant in downtown Chicago. Jake grinned. "Isn't it eye-catching? I'm tempted to keep it."

It was the opening salvo for serious negotiations, and they both knew the rules.

"Terry," Calib said to his employee, "I'll be in the office. Don't disturb us."

He led Jake to a small room in the back. It was messier than the shop, filled with odd bits of broken jewelry and tools. It didn't bother him when Calib didn't offer him a chair or a drink, either. The man had a reputation of being a miser.

"I can't give you what the watch is worth," Calib said, sitting in a wobbly wooden chair behind his desk and laying the timepiece on top of his calendar pad. "You know that."

"True." Jake nodded. He pushed aside a clutter of old drills and perched on the corner of the desk. "But your contact Jamison at the fine antique store across town will take it off your hands in a heartbeat." *Another degree of separation between him and the stolen item.*

Calib's eyes narrowed. "How did you…? Never mind." He tore a piece of paper from a notepad, scribbled on it, and passed it to Jake.

Jake knew without looking that he wouldn't accept the first offer. He crumpled the paper and tossed it on the desk. "Try again."

The pawnbroker pursed his lips and repeated the procedure. Jake played along, looked at the sheet, then picked up the Rolex and stuck it in his pocket. "I'm doing you a favor and you're not even trying."

"Hold up." Calib stood and held out his hand. "Let me see the watch? I'll check it out on the internet and figure if I can do better."

Jake had done that, but this was a standard part of the negotiations. He laid it on the desk, wishing he could keep it, but that was too risky. There wasn't any place for him to wear a Rolex without someone suspecting it had been stolen. He'd decided that's how the man at Niagara had gotten it.

He surfed on his cell phone while Calib struggled to hold his face expressionless. Jake laid odds that the pawnbroker never won at poker. It was too easy to read his unhappiness in the downturn of his lips and the slumping of his shoulders. "Well?" he asked, tired of the farce.

Calib shook his head and laid his trembling hand on top of the Rolex. "I'll never get a chance like this again."

"Dig deep. You stand to make a huge profit if you play your cards right."

"There's no evidence you took it?"

Jake shrugged. "I covered my tracks. Picked up a stone at the same time as the piece. As far as any video record, all I did was look at a rock and toss it."

"The cops are going to catch up to you one of these days."

"Then give me enough that I can take a break and get the police to lose interest in me."

Calib scrawled figures on his notepad again. His handwriting was sloppy, and Jake wasn't able to read it upside down. He hid his impatience while Calib twirled his pen and stared at what he'd written. Finally, he shoved the paper towards Jake.

The number wasn't bad, but Jake pulled a pen from his jacket pocket and wrote a new figure, adding two thousand dollars to the offer before pushing the pad back.

The notepad danced across the desk until the numbers reached a point where Jake figured he'd hit the limits of Calib's available cash. It was more than he'd hoped for, less than he'd dreamed. He wrote the same number under Calib's last offer and initialed it.

"That's going to hurt." The pawnbroker tapped his pen on his desk. "You're a hard man, Hennessey."

"I'll give you two minutes to change your mind."

One side of Calib's mouth rose. "Hard but fair. If you wait in the store, I'll get your money."

Jake slid the Rolex into his pocket. "I'll hold on to this in the meantime."

"Don't you trust me?"

Jake arched his eyebrows.

"Yeah, I'd do the same thing."


To cover his apprehension, Jake examined the small, overflowing bookcase. Were there any books that Harmony would like? The several he plucked from the shelves appeared to be science fiction, based on the rockets, green aliens, and UFOs that decorated the covers. Not her normal choice of reading material.

But on the bottom shelf, he spotted a biography about Winston Churchill. It seemed more her style. He knocked the dust off the thick volume and flipped through the pages. He'd stopped to glance at a random page when Calib opened the office door. Instead of putting it back, he carried the book with him.

Calib cocked his head when Jake laid the volume on the desk. "That's an odd choice."

Jake chuckled. "It's my cover story. I want something in my hands when I leave."

"And it doubles as a weapon."

"You're right." Jake hefted the book. "As good as a cast-iron skillet."

"I suppose you expect me to throw it into the deal."

"No." Jake reached into his pocket and pulled out a handful of coins. "What's that? A buck fifty? Write me up a receipt. If the cops stop me, I can honestly say I was shopping for books. Covers the both of us."

"I'll get Terry to give you one." The pawnbroker held out a large, unsealed manila envelope. "Do you want to count it?"

The rules of polite society dictated Jake's refusal. Jake didn't follow those rules. He undid the clasp and, as quickly as any bank teller, leafed through the bills, many of them hundreds. He counted and counted again, getting the same result. Then he slipped a ten out of the stack and laid it and the Rolex on the desk. "Those bills stuck together. You gave me too much."

"At least I'll have enough cash for supper tonight."

Jake tucked the envelope under his left arm, held out his right hand, and lied. "It's been a pleasure doing business with you again."

"You always win," Calib muttered, but shook the offered hand.


With the money wedged between the pages of the

book, Jake stepped into the sunshine. The deal had taken longer than he wanted, but the reward justified the risk. He shaded his eyes as a cop car rolled down the street and waited until it turned the corner before walking the short distance to his borrowed ride.

First order of business was to break his bounty into smaller pieces. A thousand here, a thousand there, a thousand in the house account. Nothing that would seem unusual or out of place and attract the attention of legal authorities. He'd even be able to add to his 'retirement fund,' when he got home: a stash of bills in a hidden compartment of the Charger.

If he left now and broke the speed limit most of the way, he could get to Oak Grove in time to take Harmony to supper to celebrate, a spectacularly good but simultaneously terrible idea.

"We don't accept cash," the bored desk clerk, a college-aged man, repeated, "Only credit cards. And none of those phony gift cards either."

Jake had his heart set on staying at a proper hotel instead of a shady motel. He took his overstuffed wallet out of his back pocket and opened it, as if trying to decide what he wanted to do. The clerk's eyes popped out at the sight of the fat wad of bills.

"You don't make any exceptions?" Jake pulled a fifty from the wallet and laid it on the desk.

The clerk—Peter, according to his nametag—strummed his fingers on the computer keyboard.

"It's against policy." His voice shook.

Jake added a twenty.

"The room rate is $250. You'll need a card for the security deposit," the young man said, the words tumbling over each other. "Or another $250 cash we will return if you have no damages or no charges against the room."

"My big plans for the night include a hot shower and a good night's sleep." The $250 would barely make a dent in the day's profit. He put five hundreds to the left of the other bills and added a twenty to the clerk's share.

The suite wasn't the most luxurious Jake had ever stayed in, but it was near the top of the list. He stretched out on the bed to test it and decided the only way to make it better would be to have Harmony lying next to him.

At six, he headed out to the car to bring in his duffel bag of clothes. Peter was outside smoking, and the color of the smoke revealed it wasn't tobacco. Jake plotted how to talk the clerk into sharing. The odor drifting his way held the promise of a good high.

"Is your room alright?" Peter asked politely, holding the joint by his side to hide it.

That was the opening Jake needed. "Perfect. Quiet, just the way I like it. Away from the elevators and ice machine. And the balcony is a bonus in case I need to make a quick getaway."

He delivered the line deadpan with a poker face. Peter glanced twice towards the building before responding.

"Sir, we don't have balconies. And you're on the fourth floor."

Jake grinned and winked. "Gotcha. That must be quality weed."

The clerk blinked and then smiled. He waited until a couple walked past them and went to their car. He held out his hand—the one holding the joint. "It is. Have a toke."

*  *  *

Peter had given him directions to a nearby park where Jake could buy more. Even after enjoying the smoke several times and giving a joint to Peter, he still had half an ounce left when he headed towards Oak Grove the next morning, with enough time to stop and see Harmony before going back to Atlanta. He factored in a stop at the Purple Onion, and a chance to share the weed with acquaintances who'd treated him a time or two. The rules demanded repaying favors, and it was a good way to catch up on the latest gossip. He wondered if there had been any more robberies.

Habit found him pulling into his normal motel. Jake was tempted to rent a room at the more prestigious The Towers, Oak Grove's best hotel, but he didn't want to flash his money in a town where people knew him. Muscle memory made the choice.

Harmony was at work, but Jake was too high to care. With a simple bouquet of bright yellow daisies from the local florist in hand, he dashed up the steps of the library, hoping she wouldn't spot him and ruin the surprise. Her co-worker at the front desk winked at him and pointed towards the periodical room. He nodded his thanks, slowed his steps, and did his best imitation of a cat sneaking up on its prey.

She had her head buried in a magazine, making it easy. He slipped one flower from the bunch and laid it on the open pages.

"Oh!" She lifted her face, and her mouth broke into a wide smile that wrinkled the corners of her eyes. "Jake!"

"Hey." His grin was genuine. "I have to return to the office tomorrow, but I couldn't resist stopping to see you. Can we do supper tonight?"

Her mouth wiggled, as if holding back a laugh. "Let me check my social calendar."

"It's not Wednesday, is it? Girls' Night Out? Sometimes when I have too many meetings, I lose track of the days."

She laid the magazine on the shelf, in the wrong spot, and reached up to tug on his collar. "No, today is Thursday. And yes, I'd love to go to supper with you."

"Good. Where should I make reservations?"

"Are you going to spend your afternoon at the old house?"

"I thought about patching a few spots up on the third floor." *After a quick stop at the Purple Onion.*

"Then how about the Dairy Barn? Easy and no reservations needed."

He opened his mouth to object, and she put her

finger on his lips. "The novelty of 'us' has worn off, and no one will interrupt."

He hoped. He took her hand in his and kissed each finger. "The Dairy Barn it is." How many women would be happy going to a burger place instead of somewhere fancy? Another reason he loved her.

He hadn't said that word to her, and he didn't intend to, although he'd been using it as his signature on the postcards. Harmony was too good for him and everyone but Harmony knew it. He skipped the Purple Onion and took out his frustration on the hole in the wall left by the doorknob in a third-floor room of the Victorian. A final swipe of sandpaper and he stepped back to admire his work. Not perfect, but several layers of paint would cover the flaws. Maybe there was still hope for the old house.

The patch didn't stick out from all the existing patches. No one would guess there was a treasure behind it. He'd taped a few hundreds behind the wall stud, his private version of a bank.

A faint footstep made him twirl around to make sure someone wasn't creeping up behind him. No one was there, and he laughed at himself. Harmony claimed a ghost haunted the house, but it was her imagination. Or was it?

Based on the sunlight streaming through the filthy window, he had time to patch one or two more holes. Then he'd head back to the motel and clean up before his date.

# Chapter 21

The Dairy Barn menu was always better than what the average fast-food joint offered, but with Harmony across the booth from him, Jake didn't even taste his hamburger. Behind her black-rimmed glasses, her eyes sparkled.

"After you left," she said, taking a sip of her butterscotch milkshake, "a group of ladies came in. It turned out they are romance authors from Pittsburgh. They heard about our collection of Victorian-era books and are doing research. I guided them to a few tidbits of information they hadn't known to look for."

"You had fun doing it." Jake grinned before shoving a French fry into his mouth.

"Honestly, it's the best part of being a librarian. I'd do nothing but research if I could. But there's not enough demand in Oak Grove to make it a full-time job."

"Have you ever considered living anywhere else?"

"Sure. The Smithsonian interviewed me for a position, and I almost took it. But I love this town and when the library offered me a job, I jumped on it."

"I've been to DC a time or two." His business had involved a ring with a large diamond. "It's an interesting city, but I didn't do any sightseeing. I don't have the patience to stand in line."

"I've always wanted to visit the National Library. Maybe someday."

Harmony waved, and he turned to see a little girl staring at them. Well, staring at her.

"You have a fan," Jake grinned.

"She comes in for story hour once in a while. I suspect those are her grandparents."

"I won't argue with you. If you looked up grandparents in the dictionary, they'd be the perfect illustration." The sparkling gem dangling around the grandmother's neck tempted him, but as long as they lived locally, they were off-limits.

They shared a comfortable silence while they worked on their food. Jake used the time to come up with a plan to delay the hoped-for trip to Harmony's bed. If he'd learned anything, it was that anticipation was her favorite kind of foreplay. He settled for an old standby.

"Do you want to go for a walk after this?" he asked, as they waited for the waitress to bring the one brownie they'd agreed to share.

"It's cold. In fact, we had snow last week. Do you think you can handle it?" she teased with a broad smile.

He leaned forward so his words were for her alone. "You've already got me hot. I'll keep you warm."

She waved her hand in front of her face as a deep red colored her cheeks. "Oh, my."

Jake chuckled in satisfaction.

"I'm going to need you to step away from the freezer, Jake. You're melting the ice," she said with a grin.

He should have known she wouldn't give up easily. She'd beat him at this game, but he'd make his best shot with lines he remembered from high school. "Did you just come out of the oven? Because you're too hot to handle."

The grin got bigger, and she waggled her eyebrows. "That's a nice shirt. Can I talk you out of it?"

"If you were a library book, I'd check you out," he replied, putting on his poker face.

She rolled her eyes. "I don't know whether to give you extra points for that one, because it's relevant, or take one away because I've heard it more than once. But here's mine. You're so hot, you must be the cause of global warming."

Something about a volcano and lava. Jake reached for the memory, but he couldn't grab it. He was saved by the arrival of the waitress, and the sight of the treat inspired him. "I didn't think there was anything hotter than a good brownie, but, hey! Here you are."

The server, a middle-aged woman, put the dessert plate down, followed by clean forks. Then she placed one hand on her hip and cocked her head. "I'll give you four stars for that. Start with two because that line is as old as the pyramids. Add one, because you switched it up to match the occasion. Then I throw in another star out of sympathy, because I pity the fool who thinks they can outdo Harmony in a game of wits."

Jake pulled a fresh napkin out of the holder and swung it in the air. "I surrender. It's bad enough trying to keep up with one smart lady, but I have no chance against the two of you."

Harmony giggled. "Jake, meet Melody. She's a volunteer at the library."

"Just the person I need!" He winked at Melody. "Got any secrets to keep up with her?"

"Against her, you mean?" Melody chuckled. "Nice try, but not a chance. I'm the one who has to work with her. Now, if you'll excuse me, I have other customers."

"I like her." Jake eyed the brownie, figuring out where halfway was before he cut it.

Harmony took that decision out of his hands. She cut it herself, pushing a piece towards him and taking the other half. "Don't let the fact that she's working as a server fool you. She practically runs this place."

Jake concentrated on his share of dessert. How would Harmony react if she found out that he'd been lying to her all along?

There were only a few other people in the park, but Jake limited himself to holding Harmony's hand. When he stuck his other hand into his jacket pocket, he discovered the remnants of the pot he'd bought in Cleveland. He considered dropping the baggie in a garbage can if the opportunity presented itself, but surely no one would bother them. They were only strolling down the sidewalk.

When they stopped to admire the crimson rays of the setting sun coloring the marshmallow clouds, he caught sight of a cop car cruising down the street, seemingly going nowhere in particular. It was enough to set off alarm bells.

Jake slipped his hand into his jacket pocket and opened the bag. There'd be no point in trying to dump the whole thing in a trash container. But, bit by bit, he could take out small amounts and scatter them on the breeze. The less he had on him, the more minor the charges leveled against him.

"Do you smell that?" Harmony asked as they strolled along the shore of the little pond, edged with the first spring flowers.

Jake made a show out of sniffing. "What does it smell like?"

She wrinkled her nose. "Hay? Or skunk? Or both? I can't figure it out."

"Skunks? The city keeps skunks in the park?"

She poked him in the side. "Don't be silly. But every once in a while, one wanders in from the country, and they have to set live traps to catch and get rid of it."

Two cars pulled into the parking lot across the pond. One of them appeared to be an unmarked cop car. The other was an old Mustang, but that didn't eliminate the possibility of the driver being a police informant. Was a sting about to go down and he and Harmony would become accidental participants? The odds weren't in their favor.

"What's wrong, Jake?"

The oldest excuse in the book should do. "Something isn't sitting right in my stomach. Can we head back?"

She held her wrist to his forehead. "You're not running a fever."

"That's good. But I don't want you to catch this, so let's take you home and I'll head to the motel."

They turned and started the return trip to the car, stopping once in a while so Jake could pretend that he was swallowing back rising nausea. That gave him the opportunity to get rid of more of the weed. He'd scattered all the big flower buds and had nothing but shake left when two men stepped into the path in front of them. Cops. One in uniform, one in plain clothes. And from the footsteps coming from behind them, a third. They'd brought reinforcements.

"Mr. Jake Hennessey?" the plainclothes officer asked.

Clearly a formality. "Yes. And you are, Detective?" They didn't 'feel' like the Feds, based on the rumpled brown business suit the man wore, so Jake assumed this was a local operation.

The detective arched an eyebrow. "Thomason. Detective Fred Thomason. Oak Grove Police. We have a warrant for your arrest."

# Chapter 22

"Jake?" Harmony asked, her voice trembling.

He ignored her, focusing his attention on the cops. "On what charge?"

The sun hung low on the horizon, but enough light remained in the park for Jake to read confusion on the detective's face.

"On what charge?" Jake asked again, when Detective Thomason didn't answer right away.

Thomason cleared his throat. "Possession with the intent to distribute."

"Jake?" Harmony asked again, her voice an octave higher than normal.

He turned halfway so he could look her in the eyes. "I don't sell drugs, Angel. It appears someone's given the detective bad information."

"You're the librarian?" Thomason asked. "Harmony Duprie?"

"Yes." Harmony's eyebrows knotted. "But I don't remember you. Don't you read?"

The uniformed officer covered his mouth and

coughed. Or was that a laugh, Jake wondered.

"I attended the council meeting several months ago when you spoke about the possibility of creating a tour of historical homes. City Council turned it down, but you sold me on the idea." Thomason turned to the police officer. "This can't be right."

The young cop shrugged. "That's what the paperwork says."

Jake tracked the third cop, who kept inching closer and closer to Harmony. Harmony wasn't a threat. They should be keeping an eye on him, not her.

"I'm sorry, Miss Duprie, but I have a warrant for your arrest. You're being charged as an accomplice," Thomason said.

Her jaw dropped. Jake didn't have time to comfort her. The cop behind her had palmed a little baggie filled with something white. Jake knew the drill. Slip it into Harmony's purse and then 'find' it later. That wouldn't happen when he was around, no matter what it cost him.

Jake swiveled and charged, head-first. With no time to pull his weapon, the cop crumbled under Jake's onslaught and the bag dropped to the ground. Jake stomped on it before falling on top of his victim, his fists flying. One blow mid-chest, the second lower, where it would do the most damage. Even when the other cops piled on top of him, he kept punching and kicking. No particular target, just anything he could contact. He needed to make sure there was no trace of that bag and the drugs it contained before giving up. Even Harmony's screams didn't penetrate the wall he'd erected. He'd sacrificed his future for her.

✸ ✸ ✸

"You've got yourself in a hell of a mess." Abe Donalee, the public defender, ran a finger down the top piece of paper in the stack in his hand. "Carl asked me to take a look as a favor to him, but I'm afraid there's not much I can do."

Jake winced as he adjusted the restraints that secured his arm to the hospital bed. Not an inch of him wasn't scabbed or bruised. Some injuries had been received after they'd tossed him into a holding cell. Still, it was better than being in prison. "The drug charge is bogus."

Abe, a scrawny man with thick glasses, shook his head. "Everyone knows it except for the DA, who insists on pressing charges. My theory is that it's a political play to look good for the upcoming elections. After the informant skipped town, they should have developed new leads, but didn't. You have an enemy named Ben something? He got caught trying to rob a pawnshop and offered you up for a plea deal."

And all along, Jake had thought Ben was a friend. He should've remembered his rule of trusting no one. "No. I don't know anyone named Ben. The DA dropped the case against Harmony, didn't he?"

"You mean Miss Duprie?" Abe somehow managed to smile and frown at the same time. "No, he hasn't. Half the town is ready to forgive you for beating up the cops because they figure you did it to protect her and are up in arms about it. The other half buys the story that she was part of a drug ring, even though there's no evidence, and are ready to send you to prison for life for corrupting her."

"Are you representing her, too?"

"Her? No. She doesn't need a public defender. Somehow, she's wrangled the sharpest lawyer in the state to represent her. He'll have the jury promoting her to sainthood when he gets done. The only reason the case against her hasn't been dropped is because the DA and the judge are golfing buddies. Small town politics."

"Is one of the cops that busted us related to either of them?" Jake muttered.

Abe got up and checked that the door to the room was closed. There was nothing he could do about the guard on the other side. "What do you mean?" he whispered, after returning to his seat.

"They tried to plant something on Harmony. My guess is meth." Jake shrugged, and the pain took away his breath.

"You want me to call a nurse? Get you some meds?"

Jake grimaced. "They claim I don't need them, although the cops dislocated my shoulder trying to get the cuffs on me."

"I'll see what I can do. But what's this about planting drugs? Which one?

"I didn't get names. Except for the detective, and he wasn't happy with the whole farce. It was the first cop I attacked. But no one will believe me, so don't tell anyone."

"Not even Miss Duprie?"

Jake closed his eyes, remembering the agony of

betrayal that darkened her face when they'd handcuffed her. "Especially not her. She loves this rotten little town. It will destroy her to find out what really goes on here."

"You aren't the first of my clients to make that claim. But they were known to the system, all drug users, and less reliable as witnesses. You've given me something I can take to our new police chief. Maybe he'll listen to me."

Jake reached for a glimmer of hope. "Any chance for a plea bargain based on my willingness to work with the chief?"

The public defender shook his head. "The DA is unwilling to consider any deal. No possibility for bail, either, since you're from out-of-state with limited local connections. Throw in the rumor that the FBI has been poking around, claiming you're a suspect in a string of thefts, and he's playing hardball. There's no way for me to pull off a miracle. I normally don't make predictions, and I'll do my best, but I see a prison term in your future."

❋ ❋ ❋

"The judge did me a favor and gave you a few minutes," Abe said, "while he considers your sentence. He even agreed to keep the deputies in the hallway. Don't let me down."

Jake nodded. He'd lost the ability to do more. Words would do him no good.

He sat with his hands in his lap to hide the handcuffs.

He'd tested them, and could remove them, but there wasn't anywhere for him to go. Not with two burly officers outside the door.

At least he was still in his second-best suit, the one with a lock-pick sewn into the hem, which he'd been allowed to wear for the trial. They'd missed the unfolded paper clip in the security scan, assuming it was the ankle-bracelets setting off the metal detector. He felt almost human.

When the door opened, he stared straight ahead. It wasn't Harmony, the one person he really wanted to see. She'd shown up for his trial but had avoided meeting his eyes. He'd found an unexpected ally when he scanned the courtroom—his cousin, Eli.

A body slid into the chair on the other side of the small table. "I can't get you out of this one," Eli said.

His voice was deeper than Jake remembered. The time Eli spent in the military had done him good.

Jake studied the man seated across from him. Eli had filled out. He wasn't the nerdy little kid Jake remembered. He forced words out of his mouth. "I need two favors, but one isn't for me."

"I won't make any promises."

"Hear me out. First one is easy. Take care of my car. Abe will give you the keys and the address of where it's stored. Drive it once in a while but don't have too much fun. It's a cop magnet.

"Second—and this is important—there's this lady I've been seeing. I need you to keep an eye on her and make sure she doesn't get into trouble. She's as naive as they make them. I've been able to teach her a few things, but when she's got her head in the clouds, she ignores what's happening here on earth."

Eli smiled. "Pretty, but dumb as a brick?"

Abe coughed.

"She's probably smarter than you and me combined, dweeb," Jake said, resorting to a childhood insult. "I'm worried the cops will make Harmony a target. Call it revenge."

"I sat in on her trial as much as time allowed," Abe said. "It was a joy to watch Miss Duprie and her lawyer destroy the DA's case. When they introduced into evidence a spreadsheet showing drug cases had dropped in the past year, rather than gone up as the prosecution alleged, I almost laughed. And yes, a couple of officers are unhappy their shoddy work was highlighted."

"You sold me." Eli spread his hands apart. "I'll keep tabs on the lady and help if I can."

The hard rap on the door was the sound Jake dreaded. It marked the end of any semblance of freedom. Soon they'd strip him of everything personal, the first step in breaking him. He knew the rules.

"One more thing," he added, "Don't let Harmony know. And if you have to talk to her, never tell her you're a Hennessey."

❋ ❋ ❋

The drug charges had been dismissed, but there was no escaping punishment for assaulting the officers. As Jake struggled into the prison jump-suit, he focused on the memory of the first time Harmony had pulled off a

Bootlegger's 180. The joy of accomplishment had lit her face, and she'd truly looked like an angel. He'd have no other light to sustain him for two long years in a dingy, cramped cell.

If he survived that long.

THE END

❋ ❋ ❋

Want to find out what happens to Harmony?

Take a peek at *The Marquesa's Necklace,*
Book 1 in The Harmony Duprie Mysteries

# The Marquesa's Necklace

P.J. MacLayne

# Chapter 1

I first noticed him at the other end of the row when I glanced up to find another book. I recognize most of the regular patrons, and he wasn't one of them. Curiosity kicked in, and I gave him a good looking over as I pretended to scan the table of contents of a random book I plucked off the shelf. Just because I considered myself off the market didn't mean I couldn't admire the goods, right? He wasn't the kind of man you find on the cover of romance novels, but there was something appealing about him. Enough to send a shiver down my spine—or was that the air conditioning kicking in? In any case, the truth was, I preferred a man who didn't look like he spent more time in front of a mirror than me.

The library was as quiet as a church sanctuary on a Tuesday morning—just the way I like it. As an ex-librarian, I appreciate the times when only a few patrons are perusing the shelves or racks of periodicals. Back then it gave me time to replace books or straighten out the magazines. Now that I'm a researcher for a writers' co-op, these times are when I'm most productive. None of my old coworkers object when I accumulate a large pile of books on the table I stake out as my territory for the day. They know I'll replace them in the proper places before I leave. I don't necessarily need all these books, but they create a wall I can hide behind.

I don't need to hide any more, at least not while Jake is doing time for assaulting an officer and resisting arrest, but old habits can be hard to break. Like wearing these coke-bottle glasses when I have a perfectly fine pair of contacts sitting in their case on my nightstand, or wearing my hair up in a bun. I can't count the number of times friends have tried to get me to change my hairstyle, insisting men would be more interested in me if I wore it down, but I'm not trying to attract a man. After Jake, I swore off dating.

This particular day I was deep in the stacks trying to find out what John D. Rockefeller might have served at one of his dinner parties. One of the ladies decided to set her next romance in the 1920's instead of making it a Regency. Accurate information about the regency period of England was standard fare but this was a challenge. I might even have to resort to the microfiche collection and spend hours scanning the gossip columns of the newspapers from that period. Not my favorite thing to do, but whatever. It all paid the same.

It was difficult to judge because I was sitting on the floor, but I guessed him to be taller than me. His wavy sand-brown hair was the perfect length to run my fingers through, although I had no expectation of that ever happening. His clothes—white shirt, brown slacks and brown blazer with elbow patches—reminded me of a college professor out of a movie from the 1970's. As he turned and I could see his eyes, the cell phone is my jeans pocket vibrated. By the time I looked back up from the screen, he'd disappeared.

Curiosity nearly got the better of me and I thought about asking Janine at the front desk about him, but decided against it. If word got out I'd asked about a man, the rumor mill would start churning, and I'd never hear the end of it. My plans included a quiet evening with leftover chicken casserole, a glass of white wine, and a new mystery novel I bought last weekend. I didn't want it interrupted with a dozen calls from my nearest and dearest friends.

I spent a few days peering into the microfiche machine to chase down a Rockefeller's banquet menu. That's why my contract with the co-op specifies I get paid a salary. Naturally, the lady in question changed her mind about the scene the same day I presented my findings to her, and had a different project for me. She wanted to find out about the colleges in the Bronx back then. I didn't tell her, but I had spotted a book with the information she needed during my earlier research. Off to the library I went, laptop in tow, along with a portable hand-scanner. Though it was expensive, it's saved me the cost of copies for several years now.

That's when I ran into him the second time. I was doing my normal thing of walking through the 940's with my nose in a book and I almost bumped into him. A sudden rush of cold air made me stop in my tracks and look up into a pair of eyes such a light blue they were almost gray.

"Oops, sorry about that." I reached out to stop myself from falling, but he backed away. I managed to latch onto a shelf instead, so I didn't end up with my face on the floor. My book did fall, and he bent over and picked it up. Without so much as a smile, he handed it to me and walked away without a word. Annoyed, I stood there with my mouth open and watched him turn the corner and vanish from my view. As I returned to my book I smelled the most unusual thing. I don't know if it was his aftershave or what, but it made me think of freshly-turned dirt.

I stopped to talk to Janine on my way out. I wondered what she could tell me about him. He seemed vaguely familiar, but I couldn't place where I'd seen him before. She just looked at me, shook her head and rolled her eyes while I nervously fiddled with my necklace.

"Haven't caught sight of him," she said. "You sure you aren't imagining things? It's time for you to start dating again. We'll talk about it more tonight." Great. Exactly what I figured.


Wednesday night was girls' night out at our hangout of choice, the Pink Flamingo. The Flamingo is about a quarter restaurant, three-fourths bar, and has been our favorite spot since high school. The plastic birds it took its name from have faded to an almost white color from exposure to the sunshine through the front windows, but the owner has never replaced them. Not much has changed in ten years, except we no longer sit up front in the restaurant section with its beige upholstery and bright lighting. We've graduated to the middle section where most of the seating is barstools or wooden chairs at small tables, and only a few booths line one wall and lighting is kept to a minimum. The back is reserved for pool players and their buddies.

Mid-week, the Flamingo didn't attract much of a crowd. A few regulars play pool, but we could gossip without constant interruptions from guys looking to pick us up. Of course, Merrilee was always their first target. Her long blond hair and supermodel body made her a guy magnet for the newbies. Too bad she plays for the other team. That leaves me, Janine and Sarah, all brunettes, to pick up after her when we are so inclined.

The three of us looked enough alike that people sometimes mistook us for sisters. We all had long hair, but I was the tallest with Janine and Sarah about two inches shorter than me. Our eyes were brown, but Sarah listed hers as hazel on her driver's license. Janine tends to be a little paler than the rest of us but that's because she spent more time with her nose buried in a book than even me.

But this night, no one bothered us. I think Sarah was disappointed. She dumped her last boyfriend a few weeks earlier and was in the market for a new flame. All dressed up and wearing a pair of bright red stilettos, she eyed every man that walked in, but didn't spot anyone of interest. However, right on cue, once we had our drinks but before the food arrived, Janine brought up my mystery man.

"We've got to fix Harmony up pretty soon," she giggled. "She's imagining guys now."

I took a big swig of my brown ale before answering. I blame my liking for it on Jake. He introduced me to the variety of beers, and pale ales bore me now. "You must have been in the bathroom when he came in or something, because he was there. Twice."

"Well, if he hangs out in history, maybe he's your competition," Merrilee chimed in.

I snorted, and almost knocked over my mug. Only a quick catch kept it from toppling over and spilling its contents into my lap. "If he wants to give it a try, he's welcome to it. He's probably gathering information for a college paper. Or he's a first-time author doing research for himself." Even as I said it, I decided the idea made a lot of sense. After having worked with the writers group, I know how focused they get when they're on a writing streak. My mystery man probably wouldn't even remember seeing me. I tipped my chair back, took another drink of my beer and dismissed the issue. Thank heavens, the girls got distracted by a hot guy who picked that moment to swagger into the bar.

Books in the
# Harmony Duprie Mysteries Series
P.J. MacLayne


## THE MARQUESA'S NECKLACE

Harmony Duprie enjoyed her life in the quiet little town of Oak Grove—until her arrest for drug trafficking. Now she has to figure out who is behind the sinister incidents plaguing her, and why.


## HER LADYSHIP'S RING

Harmony Duprie is back, and so is trouble in Oak Grove.

Her ex-boyfriend Jake is out of prison and a suspect in a murder. Can Harmony clear Jake's name and solve the mystery of her own heart?


## THE BARON'S CUFFLINKS

What starts as Girl's Night Out ends in murder, and Harmony Duprie is a suspect.

She's innocent, of course, but with no alibi, the sheriff's department won't remove her from the list of suspects. But caution isn't Harmony's middle name and she plunges head first into danger to defend her honor.

## The Contessa's Brooch

A firebug is stalking Oak Grove and internet researcher Harmony Duprie is on the case. It starts as a simple data analysis project for Police Chief Sorenson, but things get personal when the house she renovated is targeted.

The arsonist is in it for the glory, posting videos of his exploits on social media. Can Eli, Lando and Scotty, Harmony's favorite computer hackers, help her track down the pyromaniac before someone gets hurt? Or, worse yet, killed?

## The Samurai's Inro

Harmony Duprie has it made. Or so she thinks.
New job.
New routine.
A quiet life in the quiet little town of Oak Grove.
Oh, and Eli.

But trouble has a long memory and it's playing a deadly game.

## The Ranger's Dog Tags

It isn't the first time Eli Hennessey has disappeared. Is it the last?

Books in
# The Free Wolves Series
P.J. MacLayne


## WOLVES' PAWN
### *Book 1*

Dot McKenzie is a lone wolf-shifter on the run. Can she survive when she becomes a pawn in a pack leader's deadly game?


## WOLVES' KNIGHT
### *Book 2*

Tasha Roeper knows what it means to protect your own. Torn between tradition and a changing world, will Tasha risk everything to save a friend—including her own life—when old enemies arise?


## WOLVES' GAMBIT
### *Book 3*

Free Wolf Lori Grenville has made it her life's mission to help unhappy shifters escape from overbearing alphas and dangerous situations. She hasn't failed in a mission yet. This one may be the exception.

# P.J. MacLayne
*Can be reached at*

NEWSLETTER
eepurl.com/cL73Cz

WEBSITE
PJMacLayne.com

FACEBOOK
facebook.com/pjmaclayne

TWITTER
twitter.com/pjmaclayne

BOOKBUB
bookbub.com/profile/p-j-maclayne